To Win and to Lose

Introducing THE KILLERS, a savage new Mayflower series. The Killers are an international brigade of criminals, ex-criminals and misfits, a deadly syndicate with allegiance to no one government but with a terrible, violent vendetta against the Nazis.

To Win and to Lose

Klaus Netzen

Mayflower

Granada Publishing Limited
Published in 1974 by Mayflower Books Ltd
Frogmore, St Albans, Herts AL2 2NF

Made and printed in Great Britain by
Richard Clay (The Chaucer Press) Ltd
Bungay, Suffolk
Set in Linotype Plantin

For P.L.—not least for his excellent croûtons.

CHAPTER ONE

The Olympia was packed to the ceiling. The crowd still buzzed from Johnny Hess singing the 'Lambeth Walk' to close his act – a tribute to the numbers of men in British uniforms in the audience. The cheering had been loudest from a group of young men in Royal Air Force blue, in the middle of the stalls.

In the front row of the balcony, his chin resting on the dusty velvet rail, was a tall, thin man, with dark brown eyes and high cheek-bones. His slender fingers toyed with an unlit Gauloise cigarette. He wore a light green shirt and no tie – merely a loosely-knotted cravat with a Paisley pattern. His clothes were well-cut without being ostentatious; his manner that of an undoubted gentleman.

Slumped sideways in the next seat, half-turned as he looked at a lovely girl several rows back, was his companion. It would be hard to envisage a more different man. Indeed, had you not noticed them in whispered conversation during the intermission, then you would not have imagined they could even know each other. He was tiny, perhaps five feet two inches tall, with a deformation of the shoulder that his friends ignored and his enemies used behind his back when they called him 'Le Bossu' – the hunchback. His chin was pointed, and his eyes a startling blue. He wore faded dungaree trousers and a short-sleeved black silk shirt. Very old and torn. A keen onlooker might have noticed that both forearms carried a number of small scars – old needle tracks. The only other clue to his past or present was a heavy gold ring on the right hand, with an ornate pattern of a flying Chinese dragon engraved upon it.

The well-dressed man was called John Standish, and he was an English country gentleman, whose face was familiar to readers of Tatler, gleaming out of the society pages, as he escorted various ponderous matrons to Hunt Balls. His companion was Jean Marreq, a painter. And an assassin.

'We must be moving. We've much to do before the morning.'

Marreq turned back to face his companion. 'Not yet. She is next.'

The huge curtains swished back, barely trailing over the stage. All the lights went out, save the twinkle of the small bulbs over the music-stands of the orchestra. They struck up – crashing, heavy chords – and one single spotlight blared out across the smoky auditorium, hitting a little off-centre, then quickly adjusting to a tight cone of whiteness in the exact middle of the stage. The chords faded away, and the great theatre was silent. No one coughed or even dared shuffle his feet.

The clicking of heels across the boards, then the space of light was filled. By a tiny woman, a handful of skin and bones carelessly thrown together, with a pale face, tilted back to absorb the furious applause that greeted her appearance. She raised her thin arms, standing still in all that blackness, acknowledging the cheers.

Standish raised a pair of opera glasses to his eyes. She hadn't changed since he had last seen her, before her reputation had soared to its present height; perhaps she was a little thinner, if that were possible, and her hair seemed shorter. The applause died away and she launched into her first song.

He turned to Marreq, perched on the front of his seat, his short legs dangling. 'God, her voice!'

There was no reply from the Frenchman, his eyes fixed on the stage.

La Môme Piaf – the little sparrow – had them all in the palms of her small hands. Hair pushed back over her ears, a high-necked dress in blue – Royal Air Force blue, Standish noted – fingers dramatically accentuating the lines of her songs, she was totally in command of the theatre. Even if you knew no French, and Standish was supremely fluent, you could not fail to be touched by her presence. That mixture of aggression and vulnerability. Of frailty and power.

Standish glanced down at his watch, peering to make out the luminous numbers. It was nearly eleven. He nudged Marreq with his elbow, but the Frenchman merely waved an irritated hand at him. He shrugged and relaxed. When Piaf had done, and not before, his comrade would be ready.

The last song was appropriate, as she knew it was, and the reaction was thunderous. 'Où sont-ils mes copains?', to which the answer was that they had gone to make war. With Germany poised to make an attack at any moment, the words touched a chord for every man there. As she reached the last line – 'Où sont-ils? Où sont-ils?' – the white light winked out, and the stage was flooded with streams of coloured light – red, white and blue – while an enormous tricolour was unfurled at the rear of the stage.

Cries of 'Encore, encore' went unanswered, but Piaf came back on to the stage, to lead the entire company in a rousing 'Marseillaise'. Everyone joined in, and Standish was not surprised to feel a lump in the back of his throat. All about him, Frenchmen stood rigidly to attention, tears streaking their cheeks. It was a time to feel pride in your country.

But, the dark days were coming closer, and there was little light to the east.

Marreq and Standish drifted out of the Olympia, carried along by the chattering crowd, into the well-lit Boulevard des Capucines.

'Shall we take the Métro?'

'No, I've had enough of being crowded in with my fellow-man for one night. We might as well walk. It'll be nearly as fast at this time of night.'

Despite his lack of height, Marreq set off at a fast pace, and Standish was pushed to keep up with him. Neither spoke a word until they were bustled along the Rue Pigalle, past the Théatre des Masques, when traffic made them halt for a moment. The Englishman seized the chance to ask a question.

'Jean, why so low? I thought that you were the greatest admirer in the world of Piaf.'

Marreq spat in the gutter, narrowly missing the patent leather shoe of a waiting prostitute. She swung her feathered scarf round her neck and cursed him for a clumsy crook-back. He pivoted swiftly on his heel and smiled up at her, his eyes piercing. 'Beware, Mademoiselle. You work for the Algerian? Well, I can speak to him about a certain matter that he and I share, and he will arrange to pour a few drops of vitriol into your eyes.'

The girl went white, and made no attempt to reply. The traffic eased, and the two men crosssed. Standish looked back, and she still stood unmoving.

'I say, Jean. What's put you in such a damnable ill-temper?'

They resumed their walk, across the bustling Place Pigalle and up the quieter Rue des Martyrs, climbing towards the spun-sugar dome of the Basilique du Sacré-Coeur. Jean Marreq stopped outside a small bistro. 'I am in such a damnable ill-temper, my friend, because I love France. All those fools in the Olympia, sodden with the after-effects of Piaf, drunk on a phoney patriotism, bellowing out their hatred of an enemy they have none of them seen. They babble of letting impure blood water the furrows of their beloved France. Pah! I tell you Standish. If the Germans should reach Paris, these will be the same men who lie down and let the Nazis step on their faces.'

Again he spat on the cobbles. It was a cool spring night, with a light breeze to wipe away the heat of the day. Finally, the two men reached their goal – a shadowed house in a dingy courtyard, just off the Rue Cortot, in the heart of Montmartre. While Marreq fumbled for his key, they could hear the dismal voice of a drunk, wailing for the moon in the nearby Cemetery of Saint Vincent.

'Come on. We're late and I could do with a little wine to brace me for the work.'

'Oh, shit! Come on you bastard key! Right!' The key turned stiffly in the lock, and the door to the house creaked open. Though it was midnight, a light still glowed yellow in the room of the concierge. A figure blocked out the top half of the glass door, opening it.

'Monsieur Marreq, and Monsieur Constant. You are out late tonight?'

'Goodnight, Monsieur Corneille,' said Standish, and attempted to edge past the fat man and make his way upstairs to the rooms he shared with Marreq. Or, had shared since he arrived in Paris twelve days ago.

'Pardon me, Monsieur. Despite the lateness of the hour, I wonder whether you might like to step into my room for a talk.'

Marreq faced up to the concierge, like a mastiff against a bear. 'Monsieur Corneille, I am unable to think of any reason why I and my friend here should lose any sleep in order to engage in idle chatter with you. If you will move your over-ripe carcass from the passage-way, we will bid you good-night.'

The fat man continued to smile amiably at them, not one bit concerned by Marreq's obvious dislike. 'Come. I only wished to discuss something I noticed as I was cleaning the landing outside your rooms. I leaned – accidentally of course – against the door. Perhaps the catch was faulty. Anyway, before I knew what was happening, I had plunged through into your chambers. Imagine my surprise!'

Standish tightened his lips. 'Perhaps, Monsieur Corneille, we might avail ourselves of your kind offer of hospitality. While we discuss these amazing occurrences. Come Marreq.'

Still, the man did not move. 'One small thing. So small it desolates me to even have to mention it. But Monsieur Marreq has been a little rude about me. Some might even say, very rude. Perhaps, he might mutter an apology before we go in and talk about . . . about money.'

Marreq doffed the beret he was wearing and swept it low to

the floor. 'My deepest apologies for doubting your personal hygiene. I now realise that you would find it impossible to get any higher. Oh, in your standards, of course.'

Corneille still looked suspicious, but stood aside to let them through into his part of the house. As Marreq passed, the concierge whispered: 'Enter, Monsier le Bossu.'

Marreq's eyes narrowed a fraction, and his breath was held a moment longer than usual, but he said nothing. He knew that this was not yet the time, nor was it the place. All three men were in the room, so Corneille closed the door, and pulled down a tatty blind over the glass half of it, so that nobody could see in. Not that there was likely to be anyone around. Marreq had the top half of the house, and a deaf old colonel of cavalry the room immediately above the concierge.

Corneille offered round a packet of cigarettes and a bottle of Pernod. Both were refused.

Standish walked over to stand near the sideboard, loaded with pictures of Corneille as a young man, heavily moustached and already with a fine double chin. There was a brown-tinted daguerreotype of the concierge as a bright-eyed poilu, his rifle on his shoulder.

Corneille saw where he was looking and shrugged his shoulders. 'The war to end all wars, eh, Monsieur! Was that not what they called it? Now, we will have another. With the same suffering. But, this time General Gamelin and our precious Maginot Line will hold them back.' He took a slug at his cloudy glass of Pernod and laughed. 'So they say. All the last lot gave me was a lung full of mustard gas and a pension worth less than a tart's kiss. Fuck all generals and fuck all governments. Eh?'

The small room stank of sweat. Turning impatiently to face him, Standish snapped: 'It is late. We are both very tired and would like to get to bed. Say what you have to say and let's be done!'

Another gulp drained the glass, and Corneille sat down at the table. From the tiny kitchen behind them, came the sound and smell of frying onions. His face lop-sided from the drink, the concierge spoke with a sly smile. 'Well. When the door opened, accidentally, I thought perhaps I had better have a look around to make sure all was well. Imagine my surprise when I found great piles of money. Great piles of German money. Mountains of deutschmarks, overstamped for use in Poland!'

Marreq and Standish exchanged glances, and the hunchback moved casually round the room, until he was leaning near the door. Corneille ignored him, and continued. 'But, Messieurs, oddest of all was all this load of money was forged. Imagine that! Millions of deutschmarks, ready ... for what?'

Marreq spoke, toying with a large silk handkerchief that he had pulled from the pocket of his dungarees. 'It would be a matter of no little interest to me, to be told how you know that this money was forged?'

Wagging a finger, with a knowing grin Corneille reached for the Pernod bottle. 'Ah, little one. Papa Corneille is no fool. I see the money and I ask myself where a poor painter can have got all that. Unless his friend has brought it. So, perhaps the well-dressed Monsieur Constant is a patron of the arts. Or, perhaps he is a fucking queer who likes cripples.'

The last was said with no change of tone, which made it more bitter and more shocking. Marreq took a step towards him, mouth working. But Standish waved him back with an urgent gesture. 'Go on. Your ravings are somewhat boring, but I think you might have more to tell us.'

'Indeed I have. I took the liberty of looking through the rest of the rooms. In the cistern of the toilet, I found a set of printing plates, wrapped in rubbered cloth.'

The glass was a quarter-full with the light yellow liquid, and Corneille got up and lurched through to the kitchen for water. He brought back a cracked jug and poured from it, watched silently by the two men, into the glass. The clear Pernod instantly assumed that magical misty quality, and he drank deep.

Standish sat down across the table from him. 'What will you do? Before you answer, let me just tell you this. My friend and I have indeed forged that money, but it is intended to be passed into occupied Poland to help ruin the economy the Nazis are trying to set up there. There will be little money in it for us.'

Corneille laughed disbelievingly. 'What? You do it when there is little money and great risks! I say that you are a liar. You are a couple of cheap crooks.'

'I ask you again. What will you do?'

The rest of the glass followed the first. 'I am not rich, Monsieur Constant. I can't afford nice clothes like you. So, I think you might pay me to keep my mouth shut. If you don't pay me, then I will be straight round to the police and tell them of the international forgers I have discovered. I reckon there might be a fair reward for you.'

Standish sighed. 'In that case, there really isn't much we can say. I am truly sorry. Jean!'

Corneille looked up as the smaller man slid from his position near the door, the silk handkerchief now wrapped tightly around his knuckles. He put his hands on the table, palms down, and began to press against the scarred top, ready to rise. He was a big man, and Marreq was very small. And a hunchback.

Jean's hand flicked out twice, slapping Corneille hard across the face. He felt the sting on his cheeks and put his hand up to rub the place. 'Fucking Jesus and Mary! You fucking little swine! You've cut me!'

Bright red blood flowed down his face from two deep cuts, pouring through the stubble on his chin, dripping on to his neck, soaking his shirt. Veinous blood, released by Marreq's blows. A lifetime in Monmartre had given the small man training in every trick of the apache. For years the razor had been a favourite weapon of the Paris thugs, until increased pressure from the flics had made it too dangerous to carry. So, someone discovered that a piece of silk, pulled tight round the fist, would cut a man's face to the bone as neatly as the finest razor.

Corneille staggered back, horror on his face, his hands waving feebly at Marreq. Standish had been ready for the attack and had moved instantly around the table, so that he stood on the other side of the concierge, slightly to his left. Stiffening his hand, fingers rigid, Standish struck once at the man's groin, feeling the board-like edge of his palm crush into the softness. Felt it grate against the pubic bone.

There was a strangled scream, high and thin like a gelded stallion, then the concierge collapsed retching to the floor, his hands clutching at his groin. In his agony he looked up at Standish, breath rasping in his throat.

Marreq looked across at Standish, held his eyes for a moment. Questioning. He glanced down at the writhing figure, then nodded. Jean swung his right foot back, then sharply forward, aiming at the back of Corneille's neck, just below the ear. There was the tearing sound of cartilage and splintered bone as the neck broke. The man was dead from that moment, though the wrecked nervous system kept the arms and legs twitching like a landed fish for several seconds after.

Standish and Marreq stood and watched the corpse. Apart from the soft scrabblings of finger-nails on the worn lino, there was silence.

'Jean. Go in the kitchen and turn off those onions. I think they're beginning to burn.'

CHAPTER TWO

'First, having cleaned out the fowl, cut the bird into half a dozen pieces. Heat together in a pot three level tablespoons of butter, a quarter pound of diced breast of pork – do try to get the meat as lean as you can – and a few small onions. When this has browned slowly, put in your chicken with a finely crushed clove of garlic and a quarter pound of mushrooms. Bring the heat up and cook till golden-brown. Don't forget to keep the lid on. When it's done, take off the lid and skim away the fat. Pour over a small glass of brandy and flambé. Then pour on a pint of good wine, from Auvergne. That's important. The wine must come from Auvergne. Preferably the Chanturgne. After brisk cooking for twenty minutes, take out the chicken and pour over the sauce we discussed earlier, thickened with the chicken's blood mixed with crushed liver and a little more of the brandy. And there it is. A real old-fashioned recipe for that dish of dishes – coq au vin. I hope you enjoy it. And with it? What better than some more of that beautiful wine from the Auvergne. A fine red Chanturgne. That concludes the Monday Meal. Roland Calder will be with you in a moment to give a round-up of news and views from the free countries of Europe. Until then, here's some music from the B.B.C. Overseas Broadcasts Department. Saint-Saëns' 'Danse Macabre'.'

A sharp click as John Standish reached over and turned off the radio. His aquiline face was lined and weary. The night's work had been hard, and had continued until half an hour ago. All the forged money was packed away in three suitcases, and the plates were hissing and bubbling in a flat dish of acid.

Two floors below them, the body of the concierge, Georges Corneille, was already stiff and cold, congealed blood matting his hair. His unexpected intervention had forced the two men to bring their plans forward by twenty-four hours. That had been bad enough, but it wasn't disastrous. But now came the radio broadcast they had listened anxiously to.

Standish put down his mug of black coffee untasted and frowned. 'Fucking Chanturgne! And they repeated it. Someone over there must be really wetting their knickers. I'll have to go straight back this afternoon, Jean. I'm sorry to leave you with so much shit to clear up, but it must be pretty bloody urgent.'

The Frenchman waved his hand deprecatingly. 'Please, John. I beg that you don't even give it another thought. We've packed up all of the money and I can arrange for a little help this end to get it moving. Then it's all up to Zbigniev.'

'What about removing the garbage from downstairs?'

Marreq got up and walked across to the dish of acid. The plates were nearly dissolved, and the liquid was almost still. An occasional bubble rose languidly to the surface and lay there greasily. 'I will use my palette knife and spread some of this over Monsieur Corneille's revolting features. After a little he will begin to resemble the portrait of Dorian Gray. Once the eyes and face have melted away like the morning dew, I will perform a small amount of surgery on his mouth. A few smears of this acid on the tips of his fingers. That is all it will take.'

Standish picked up the coffee again and took a sip, cursing at the heat. 'Jesus wept! Are you sure you haven't put the plates in coffee and served me acid?' He sucked in breath to cool his mouth. 'Anyway, when you've performed this treatment on Corneille, what will you do with him?'

A thin smile crept across Marreq's face, paused briefly at his mouth, then disappeared. 'I will load his pockets with cobbles and then arrange for him to go for a little swim.'

Putting down the mug, Standish looked around the flat for a railway time-table. The radio message meant that something urgent had come up for him at home in England. A job of some kind for the loosely-knit organization that he headed.

Throughout Europe, a small number of professional criminals and ex-criminals had banded together to fight the growing threat of the Axis powers. All of them had some good reason to hate the Germans and their allies – Marreq's sister had been visiting friends in Warsaw when she had been caught out after the curfew by some Nazi stormtroopers. They had dragged her back to their barracks and stripped and raped her. The girl, who was only sixteen, had been so shocked and shamed by her experience that she had become a prostitute. Two months later – before the frantic Marreq had been able to track her down – she found that she was pregnant as a result of the mass-rape. She invited a German officer back to her wretched apartment with her and cut his throat with an open razor. Then, leaving a note for her brother, she opened the veins in her wrists and bled to death.

Marreq was typical in that his hatred of the Axis outweighed even his desire for life. There were others in other countries, even in Germany itself, and their acts of sabotage and assassination had earned them the name of 'The Killers'. Their numbers were so small that there was little risk of their being infiltrated or betrayed. They made their attacks at planned intervals, and only at targets that local resistance groups couldn't get to. The message over the radio from England meant that the British Intelligence Service was in grave need of help.

So, the money distribution would have to be left to Marreq, who would also need to look for a new studio to carry on his painting. John Standish left Montmartre just after midday and was in London by early evening. It was not a comfortable journey, for the train and the boat were both crowded with refugees and with British officers going home on leave.

He went straight to his club and made one telephone call. To an unlisted number. The conversation was brief and consisted only of three letters.

A light dinner was brought to his room by one of the aging

club servants, who told Standish about his son who was with the British Expeditionary Force in Belgium. The weather was warm after the crippling winter, and Standish threw his window open to breathe in the spring air. With it came the noise of the Saturday crowds thronging nearby Piccadilly. Leaving one glass of the hock in the bottle to aid him to sleep, he turned on the radio.

The news wasn't good – earlier that week the Finns had accepted Russian terms for peace. The ring of steel was gradually drawing closer about free Europe. After the news, Standish left the radio on quietly, enjoying some soft music, while he stripped and did a strenuous series of exercises.

Panting slightly from the exertion he went for a brisk shower. Later he lay in the bed, reading a few pages of the latest Raymond Chandler mystery – an American writer of whom Standish was extremely fond. He was aware of the sentimental words of one of the latest popular songs, echoing the hopes of so many Britons that the war would not come closer to England than it had already, and that it would all be over by the summer. A hope that Standish shared, but found wholly unbelievable. He knew that Hitler would not stop at Poland, any more than he had stopped at any stage. France and the Low Countries would be next for the German 'lightning war'.

And, so he slipped into sleep, still hearing the words of the song. 'But, I know we'll meet again some sunny day.' At least it made a change from the jingoism of 'There'll Always Be An England', that had been so popular at the end of the previous year.

It was Saturday, March 16th, 1940.

'I wouldn't risk the mashie, Tristram, if you don't mind a little friendly advice.'

'Why on earth not? Seems an obvious mashie shot to me. Anyway, I'm not sure I'd take anything from you. Except money, you tricky devil.'

Standish grinned at the red face of Tristram Bowditch, eldest son of Lord Abbotsford and a long way from being the fool he looked. He was Standish's contact at Military Intelligence and the two men had enormous respect for each other. Bowditch's only weakness was that he could never resist John Standish's unusual sporting wagers. The occasion that he had lost at croquet at Hurlingham with Standish using a coal hammer instead of a mallet still rankled, and he had expected to do better this time.

A second phone call, at a set time, had resulted in an agreement to meet at a certain golf club, not fifty miles from the statue of Eros, with Bowditch using a full set of clubs and Standish allowed to use only his putter.

They were now approaching the fifteenth green and Standish was four holes up. The fifteenth was a four hundred and thirty-five yard, par five hole and both men were near the middle of the fairway – Bowditch a good forty yards ahead – after two shots.

'Because, Tristram, if you use the mashie, the way you've been hooking today, you'll land in Charybdis over there and take three with your damned niblick to get out.'

Bowditch looked thoughtfully at the twin bunkers that guarded the green. 'Tell you what, John. A tenner that I beat you on this hole?'

'Done. On one condition.'

'What's that?'

Standish smiled. 'On condition that you play your next shot with a mashie.'

Swinging the club confidently, Bowditch addressed the ball. The hiss as the club descended and the solid thunk as it made contact with the ball, sending it arcing towards the green. At first it seemed destined for the right-hand bunker – Scylla – but it straightened. Bowditch grinned happily.

But, his jaw sagged as the ball hooked late towards the left and vanished over the lip of Charybdis.

'Hell, blast and bloody damnation!'

'Jolly tough luck, Tristram. That's a tenner you owe me.'

Standish walked back to where his ball lay, just behind an enormous tussock of grass. Eyeing his lay, Bowditch looked a little happier.

'Remember that I said first one down, old boy. You've still got a fair way to go – if you'll pardon the pun.'

There was no reply from Standish, who stood over his ball, eyed the green quickly and struck a fast, low swing with his putter. The ball went straight and very quickly, never more than four feet from the ground, between the two bunkers, pitching near the edge of the green and rolling to a stop about ten feet from the hole.

Bowditch, who had nearly reached the bunker while Standish played his shot, stood as one stricken, then generously applauded a remarkable golf shot. 'Bloody good. You ought to take this up for money.'

'I have,' remarked Standish drily.

Bowditch flapped out of the bunker at his first attempt, but only succeeded in sending the ball scudding over the cropped turf to finish thirty feet from the pin on the other side of the green. Standish duly holed his putt and that was that. Five and three.

'Come and give me a bit of help smoothing out the sand in Charybdis, there's a good chap. Then we can repair to the clubhouse for a noggin or two of Harry's best.'

For a minute or two, they raked absently at the disturbed sand, then Bowditch looked up at the sky. From past experience, Standish knew that the reason for their meeting was about to be revealed.

'Lovely day, John. Nicest day of the year, I'd say. Just look at that blue sky, eh! I say, isn't that a falcon?'

High above them the hawk swooped and rolled, riding the warm currents of air. Stopping raking, Standish eased himself on to the grass bank and lit a cigarette, offering one to Bowditch.

'Thanks, old man. I like this course, you know. Though

you'd hardly guess it. Played here before all this business started, with a fellow I was at school with. Leslie Peters. Don't think you know him. No? Anyway, he's done a bit of work for me here and there, and he seems to have got himself into a spot of trouble with the Boches.' Bowditch stopped talking and lay back, drawing on his cigarette. Standish watched the small white clouds bustling about the sky.

'Where is he?'

'Poland. He was trying to organize resistance groups. Right from the start, Peters was in there. Even at that meeting at the Polish Savings Bank last year. He's got a lot of the names of S.O.E. members in Poland, and now Jerry's got him. Our information – it came through Special Operations Executive high frequency two days ago – is that Peters was picked up by a dawn raid of the Gestapo on what had been regarded as a safe house. They're holding twenty men in all. Apparently, they don't yet realize they've got one of our chaps. Once they do, I doubt if Peters will be able to hold out for long. Then . . .' He let the rest of the sentence fall away, and hang between them.

'So. Won't he kill himself?'

'Good God, John! You're a bloody cold fish sometimes. Do you think it's that easy to kill yourself?'

Standish paused for a moment, watching a tiny vole that had just scratched its way laboriously to the surface, and now hesitated, blindly sniffing the air. 'Lobkowitz said, quite rightly, that it is easier to kill a friend than an enemy, and it is easier to kill oneself than it is to kill a friend. It's all a question of opportunity, Tristram. That's all. If one has the enemy, and a weapon, then it can always be done.'

The word 'done' had a slight stress, as the lean figure blurred into action. A hand reached under the left arm and whipped out holding a silvery sliver of steel. The leaf-bladed knife flashed across the bunker and pinned the vole to the turf, clean through the middle of its velvety little body.

'Like that. I often wish the Germans and their arse-licking

comrades had just one neck, so that I could slit it. Not an original thought, but I mean it.'

Though it was a beautiful, warm day, Bowditch shivered at the chill in Standish's voice, and the veil of ice that had lowered over his eyes. The short hairs at the back of his neck rose at the sure and certain knowledge that this man would kill anyone who stood between him and an enemy.

'John, you've never told me why you ... why you're so against Jerry. I know they're a load of animals and we all know old Adolf's as mad as a hatter. You told me about your French chum, and his sister wasn't it? But, you never said why ...'

Wiping his knife on the short grass, Standish kicked the corpse of the vole down into the sand, then turned and grinned at Bowditch. The tension had drained away from his face, and he was himself again. His eyes were placid, brown pools, and the tautness had gone from the muscles of the face. It was again the mask of a well-bred and somewhat idle English country gentleman. Used only to hunting, shooting and fishing, with no enemy more dangerous than a gaffed pike or a winged partridge to be faced.

'Why do I have little love for the Germans? Remember Edward Mallory?'

'By Jove, yes. My father was at school with him. If it hadn't been for a dicky ticker, he'd have gone with him to Everest on the climb of twenty-four.'

'Well, I hate the Germans simply because they are there. That's all.' He walked away over the brow of the trap, shouting back over his shoulder, 'Hurry up, there's a good fellow. At this rate we'll have to be back in town for dinner without the chance for a proper drink. Tell you what. I'll play the last three holes with my putter but I'll use the end of the handle like a cue once I'm on the greens. Tenner a hole. Well?'

Bowditch scrambled up after him, slipping on the seat of his immaculately-cut plus-fours in the process. 'I'll do better. If I don't win all three holes, I'll buy dinner at any club you name. You can't win all the games all of the time; John. It's just not cricket. If you see what I mean.'

A nineteen-twelve port finished the dinner off in perfect style. Though the cuisine had been as good as before the war, the tone was subdued. No debs threw bread rolls at their Guards' escorts, and even the music seemed muted. For much of the meal, Tristran had brought Standish up to date on the latest Whitehall talk. It was generally known that Chamberlain would not last out the year. His health was deteriorating fast. 'Cancer. That's my guess.' Tristram had whispered.

Hitler was poised to walk into the rest of Scandinavia at any moment, and it seemed there would be nobody in power capable of stopping him. Halifax was the man tipped to take over. 'Not bloody likely, Tristram. The man we need is Winston Churchill. Get the people together. Why, he even looks like a bloody bulldog!'

As they sipped moodily at the port, Standish tried to cheer up his friend. Though he always responded to requests for assistance from the S.O.E., it was mainly on account of his long friendship with Bowditch.

'Come on, Tristram. We can always go on to Mrs. Protheroe's. She's bound to have some new girls in, and she serves bloody fine sherry.'

'I can't walk all the way down to Half Moon Street just now, if you don't mind. Waste of time, anyway. Doubt if I could even raise a smile. Listen John, don't piss me about. It's too important. Peters is vital if the resistance in Warsaw isn't going to be wrecked over-night. Know how they kill underground men in Poland? Loop of piano wire round the neck, then just hang them on a butcher's hook and let them kick. When can you start?'

For a moment, Standish sat immobile, fingers of his right hand drumming on the damask cloth. 'Marreq will be back in two days. I should be in Warsaw in four days from now. That'll be March twenty-first. Saint Benedict's Day.'

Even that did little to brighten Bowditch's dolorous countenance. 'Polish is among your languages, isn't it?'

'Yes. Not as good as my Spanish, but a damn sight better than my Mandarin.'

Slurping a bit at the last of his glass of port – his seventh such glass that evening – Bowditch finally grinned. 'I bet you didn't know I knew any Polish did you? Well, just listen to this. W ubikacji nie ma papieru toaletowego!' And he smirked proudly. 'A little lady I used to know in coding told me that.'

'Did she tell you what it meant?'

'Yes. She said it was a very flattering comment about ... well, about the length of ... of my John Thomas.'

Standish threw back his head and bellowed with laughter, the sound turning heads all around the dimly lit club. The band missed a beat, then plodded stolidly on.

'God, Tristram, you really take the bloody cake. You honestly do. Length of your cock!' And he banged his head on the table in helpless merriment.

Bowditch bristled. 'I don't see it's that funny. Anyway, what does it mean?'

'What you said was "There's no toilet paper in the lavatory." Length of your cock!'

CHAPTER THREE

In the basement of a tottering house on the Rue de la Ferronnerie, close enough to the pavilions of Les Halles market for the rats to be a threat to young life as well as to property, Jean Marreq was making love.

'Darling, sweetest pearl. Oh, Lise, your thighs are twin pillars hiding a temple of Arcadian wonder. Allow me to pry a little between those pillars that I might defame that temple by my gross presence.'

The girl, a chubby tart, shared the room with an Algerian girl dying of consumption. She was out at the moment, trying to earn enough francs to buy cocaine, to take away the pain. So, Lise used the moment to entertain one of her string of lovers who paid for her favours only when they could afford it. Today, her good deed was Jean Marreq.

'Jean, my dearest lover. If you root around down there with your long nose any more I might forget myself.' This was followed by a moan, and a convulsion of the legs that showed Marreq had homed in on his target with exquisite aim and was using his tongue to good effect.

He felt her stomach muscles fluttering as she neared her climax, her thighs contracting to hold his head as tightly as any vise. Her orgasm broke about him like a hot, wet whirlpool. He still heard her scream with delight although his ears were effectively blocked. Leg muscles twitched involuntarily as the wave of passion slowly receded and her breathing slowed.

Lise reached down and tugged him up to lie on her vast expanse of breasts. 'Little Jean. I swear that you are the best. Even if you do talk a bit funny.'

Rolling one dark nipple between finger and thumb, Marreq leered up at her. 'Funny! I have never in my entire life supposed that the way in which I chose to express myself was anything other than the correct way. Perhaps I should return to my venerable teacher of elocution and learn other ways to put my tongue to good effect.'

Brains were not Lise's strong point and it was a full half-minute before the double-entendre penetrated the murky corridors at the back of her brain. When she got it she laughed so immoderately that she farted, and then began to giggle apologetically.

'My lovely innocent. Please don't think another thought about your slight indiscretion. When I perform at my best for ladies, it has not been unknown for them to crap themselves.'

That thought produced an even louder fit of giggles from Lise, which ended with a long, sweaty cuddle and a slide down the creaking bed.

The blankets humped and shook as the girl slid further and further towards the bottom of the bed, repaying Marreq's good deed for her. Silence, broken only by the steady sound of sucking, came to the room.

'Jean?' The voice was muffled.

'What is it, fire of my loins?'

'That friend of yours. The tall thin one. I haven't seen him for some time.'

'Lise, my angel of radiant mercy. If you don't do something, part of me will catch its death of cold. If you must use your mouth for the old-fashioned practice of speech, at least contrive to wrap your magically tender fingers about me.'

The apartment was split in two by a thin board partition, painted a slightly queasy shade of lemon.

An even movement rocked the bed. 'Better. Not as good. Like a draught of rough Bordeaux after an afternoon sipping the delicate essence of wormwood. Why are you concerned for the well-being of Monsieur Constant?'

'No reason at all, Jacques. Aaaagh!'

The hunchback had reached down under the bedclothes and grabbed the girl by the lobes of the ears, digging in his sharp fingernails, and twisting. Wriggling adroitly round, he managed to get astride her, kneeing her hard in the stomach to shut her up.

'Little Lise! Lying Lise! Loving Lise! You have a friend in the Gendarmerie. You've been seen going for a coffee at the Quai des Orfèvres, with that rather right-wing Inspector Maillot. Now, my dove, all I want to know is why. I give you my deepest word of honour that not the least harm will come to you. Not one hair on your adorable head will be harmed.' A cold note came to his voice, and he pressed his index finger deep inside Lise's ear, drawing blood and causing severe pain. 'The truth.'

A thread of blood inched down the girl's chin, where she had bitten into her lip with the hurt. Her eyes were wide with shock. When she managed to find her voice, it was high, unnatural. The breath came in harsh gasps as the weight of Marreq dug into her chest.

'Jean. Please! Oh, Holy Mary, the pain. I can't think.'

Marreq sprang unexpectedly off her and sat on the side of the bed, seeming suitably contrite. He didn't look at Lise at all, simply staring at the thin partition between the two halves of the room. 'Lise. My child. How could I have hurt you? Please stop! Please! I beg you not to weep. All I ask of you is that you tell me why you have been seeing this man, and what silly questions he has been asking. Then, I promise you, I will not hurt you in such a thoughtless way again. Here, wipe your lovely eyes on the edge of this sheet. Now, tell me.'

Lise sat up on the bed, her sobs gradually fading away. 'Jean. I'm sorry. Only Maillot was nice to me. You know I can never say "No" to anyone who's kind to me. All he wanted to know was about Monsieur Constant, and about a friend of his who had a room in Montmartre. But, it can't have been you because your room is near St. Germain-des-Prés. Isn't it? Well, it can't be anything to do with you. But he said that a ... someone like you and a tall thin man had been seen around. And, since he knew you, and knew that I knew you....'

The voice trailed away to nothing.

Marreq smiled at her. His mouth split so wide that it threatened to tear completely away from the rest of his face. But, his eyes didn't smile at all.

'So. You told him about Constant? About he and I? About when he came to Paris? About how you joked saying that he sometimes sounded like an Englishman?'

At each question, the girl nodded miserably. 'But, Jean. He was so interested. I told him about your apartment over the river, and how your sister had been killed and what a nice person you were. He said he'd heard of you and he would like to meet you. What's the right address for you; I didn't know and he said he wanted to talk about your sister and Monsieur Constant. He thought he might be an old friend. He's coming here later and ... Oh!'

'What time?'

Lise wheeled away from him and sat on the opposite edge of the bed, her feet on the floor. 'I wasn't to tell. But, because I like you too Jean, I'll arrange for you to meet. He'll be here in two hours.' She stood up. 'Now, I must get this place tidy. He hates untidiness.'

Marreq, still naked, his humped shoulder grotesquely shadowed and pale, crawled across the bed towards her, like some bizarre, gambolling crab. 'First, my sweetheart, you have left a little unfinished business. As I told you before. I have always believed that the soft lips of a beautiful woman are for kissing, for sipping ice-cold champagne, and for this.' He pointed down to his blatant erection, out of proportion for such a short man.

Reluctantly, Lise climbed back and lay beside him. Before taking him again in her mouth, she looked up at him, rolling her eyes in what she fondly hoped was a coquettish manner. 'And my darling won't hurt his pet dove, will he?'

Marreq relaxed and let het get on with it. 'No. Your darling won't hurt you again. I so swear.'

But his eyes watched the half-open door in the partition, as though he expected someone.

When he came, there was little external evidence, apart from the odd fact that his eyes blinked very rapidly for a few moments. He gave a deep sigh, then spoke. Not to Lise. To the man who had passed through the door barely a minute ago. Who had raised an eyebrow at the activity, and asked a silent question. Who had paused at Marreq's barely perceptible nod.

'Very well, John. You were quite right. He's coming later.'

Standish moved easily, like a hunting cat, and grasped the girl by the back of the neck as she sat up, shocked by the sudden interruption. His fingers closed round her windpipe, middle fingers digging into the laryngeal nerve, crushing the larynx. His thumbs locked behind the neck, giving the pressure he needed to pull his fingers deep into the centre of Lise's throat.

Marreq moved hastily out of the way as her hands clawed at the air. Her eyes burst from her skull with the swelling agony, and her tongue protruded darkly from her gaping mouth. Breath rasped deep in her chest, fighting for release. His face calm, his eyes as disinterested as though he were listening to a dull piece of Liszt, Standish tightened his grip, closing off the air, wrenching the head back. Just before she died, Lise's face was tugged so far back that she was looking directly into Standish's eyes. But, it is doubtful if she was still capable of seeing anything. Even recognizing the face of the man who was murdering her. Of Monsieur Constant.

'Shit! Now we'll have to clean up this mess.'

At the moment of death, all the muscles of the body relax. Lise had fouled herself, staining the already filthy bed. Standish stepped back, his face showing no emotion at having just pushed a girl into eternity. He wiped the sweat from his hands, checking to see that there were no fragments of skin under his neatly trimmed nails.

'You took your time, Jean. I've been kicking my heels in that cupboard for over an hour. Still, I suppose that I couldn't really have spoiled the last bit of pleasure for that child. I was right, wasn't I?'

Marreq busily wrapped the body in the sheets, heaving the bundle into a corner, and piling blankets on top. 'Yes. Yes, you were entirely correct, my friend. But, I trust that you will not misunderstand me when I say that I would have been more jocund if you had been wrong. She has paid a very high price for a very small piece of silliness.'

The window was stuck fast from years of misuse, and Standish gave up the struggle to try and open it. 'I regret, sometimes I bitterly regret, that one can never afford to take chances. I agree with you. It would be easy to make a futile gesture and leave money to have her buried and for masses to be said. It would not help her. And, it might again put our lives and our venture into hazard. Remember the words of Lobkowitz: "In a total conflict, one must take care not to confuse ignorance and innocence." The girl would have betrayed us to that Nazi sympathizer, Maillot. Now, he too must die. I think that it will be better to do it here.'

'We will have to wait here until he comes, with that,' pointing to the untidy bundle, already beginning to smell in the warm air of late afternoon.

'Yes. No. You're right. He would smell it. You know him, by sight? Right. Go and wait in the street, out of the way. When he comes in, follow him. If he hesitates outside, kill him instantly. I'll wait here.'

Marreq couldn't wait to get the rest of his clothes on and leave the room. Behind him, Standish sat down on the floor of the smaller chamber, closed his eyes, and slipped into a light sleep. A study of the teachings of the eleventh century Chinese mystic and poet, Tao Chu-Wen, had shown him ways to take his mind away from the present, yet keep it ready, coiled like a fine spring, for instant action. For Standish, the heat and the odour were no longer there.

Slowly, the afternoon wore on. Outside, the noises of shoppers and the sound of traffic were muted by the closed window. A large blowfly, wings iridescent in the dusty beam of sunlight, hummed angrily at the heap of bedclothes. Knowing from the smell that it contained food, yet unable to reach it.

Only once did Standish move. The light crept about the room until it reached the corner where he sat, shining into his eyes. Carefully, so that he would not be seen from the street, he eased the net curtains across. The light dimmed, turning the room into a muted cavern, far below the sea, with shimmering half-shadows.

Time passed.

A gentle vibration, hardly moving the air, as the front door of the house was opened, then closed firmly. Feet quietly descending the stairs. Standish slid easily awake, standing ready behind the door. A moment's doubt that there had been no noise of the front door opening a second time. A gentle rapping at the door, slightly muffled as though the fingers were gloved.

'Lise? Are you there?' The voice as soft as velvet, with the unmistakable accent of Provence.

Standish waited, poised on the balls of the feet, his hands extended in the classic Kung Fu fighting position. The door opened a couple of inches, then, without the least warning, crashed back violently, throwing Standish into the wall. He recovered to find himself looking into the barrel of a small automatic pistol.

'I see you admire the Germans so much, Inspector, that you even use one of their guns.'

'Before exchanging pleasantries, Monsieur, would you raise your hands above your head and face the wall. I have a little knowledge of savate myself.' His ears straining for any sound that would tell him Marreq was around, Standish slowly did as he was told.

When a man has a Mauser automatic pointed at your stomach, you will be a fool – not a hero – if you attempt any sudden move. The Hsc Auto had a notoriously light trigger.

He felt the barrel bore into his spine, while leather-gloved fingers butterflyed over his body, searching for weapons.

Though they probed firmly into both sides of the groin, they missed the slim sheath under the left arm. Which gave a tiny glimmer of hope.

'Turn round again, please, Monsieur . . . ? Monsieur . . . what? I think we would be happier if we knew each other's names. Though I am flattered that you seem to know me.'

'My name is Constant, as you well know. And, since I have made myself an authority on vermin, I know you as Maillot. A man who waits only for the arrival of the Germans in your country.'

Maillot sat down on the bed, his heavy body making the springs creak protestingly. His face wrinkled, and he sniffed suspiciously. 'Shit! What's that appalling smell? It's like an opened grave. What's that?'

He pointed at the bundle in the corner. Blood had soaked through from internal hemorrhaging and dried in a thin crust on the faded linoleum. Waving Standish back, Maillot stepped over to investigate. Tugging at the blankets, he managed to unroll the mess inside. The stench was horrific in that small, hot room. Finally, he reached the middle; with a flop, the body rolled out, face up, the eyes open, the mouth gaping. Although swollen and nearly black, it was still recognizable.

'Lise!!!' The cry was shrill, almost a scream. An obscenity from the mouth of such a big man. In his shock, Maillot let the Mauser wander from its target, and Standish saw the moment.

His left hand dashed away the gun, chopping at the wrist of the policeman. The gun went spinning into the corner, splintering a rose-painted chamber-pot on the way. His right hand lashed upwards, aiming for the nose. But, Maillot was quick. He swayed back, at the same time throwing a savage punch at Standish's groin. In turn, he moved back, and the two men circled each other warily, feinting a blow or a kick. Both were masters of oriental fighting and neither would give the other a chance. The gun lay neglected on the floor, by the frail lacquered table. On the table, a half-empty bottle of vin rouge, and a large steel corkscrew.

Both ignored the gun, for a move to try and pick it up must inevitably lay an opening for a kick. So, they weaved about each other, manoeuvring for the one chance that could prove decisive.

'Constant! Time is on my side. My men know where I am and will come within minutes.'

Standish grunted his disbelief, watching the other's eyes for the first warning of a move. 'Liar! Even a man as low as you would not wish his officers to know he was consorting with a slut.'

Suddenly, horrifically, Standish's foot slipped in the trickle of drying blood and he stumbled backwards, his foot coming down on the naked stomach of the corpse. With a savage snarl of triumph, Maillot leaped after him. A hard blow into the stomach winded Standish, and threw him on to his back. The Frenchman jumped on top of him, knees crushing his chest.

Feeling fingers scrabbling at his eyes, Standish turned his head and grabbed at Maillot's throat. Tangled in the stinking blankets, the two men fought with all the savagery of cornered animals. Feet, hands, teeth and nails were all used. The table went flying, the bottle smashing and the corkscrew tinkling across the room. Standish felt broken glass tearing into his back as he tried to press the heavier Frenchmen off his chest.

Sweat streamed down both men's faces, making it more difficult to get any sort of grip. Sick pain shot through Standish's stomach as Maillot managed to get his knee into his groin. The blanket wrapped itself over his face and he was temporarily blinded. Unconsciously, Standish was crooning low in his throat, the fight blotting out everything else in his mind.

He found a finger in his mouth, tearing at his lips, so he dug his teeth into it. Flesh parted and he bit with a dreadful ferocity, finally feeling the bone crack. Maillot screamed and seized him in a bear-like hug, his own teeth searching for Standish's throat.

The men were locked like that when the window screeched

protestingly upwards, the sound drowned by the grunting and wrestling. For a moment, Marreq – for, of course, it was he – watched, trying to distinguish man from man, man from blanket, blanket from corpse. The gun was hidden under the bed, but it's doubtful if the hunchback would have gone for it. Noisy things, guns, and not always reliable. Marreq was a creature of the dark, and his weapons were the silent weapons of stealth.

He picked up the steel corkscrew.

And bent over the fight. Watching, like a matador, seeking the moment of truth. Holding the corkscrew poised in his right hand.

For a moment, Maillot's head appeared out of the shambles, lips pulled back from his teeth in a hideous rictus of hatred and fear. Marreq shot out his left hand, like the claws of a crab and held the Frenchman's neck, pinning it to the slippery floor. Maillot's left ear was pressed hard to the lino. His right ear was an inviting, pink cavern.

Unbelieving, Maillot's eyes swivelled upwards, straining to see who it could possibly be that had interrupted the tête à tête. Seeing that gently smiling face, he froze, trying to focus on the shining object in Marreq's hand. Beneath him, Standish felt the body go rigid, and still. For a moment, he too was still.

The tableau froze, as though trapped in crystal. A timeless fraction of time, where all movement ceased. Specks of dust floated and whirled in the pools of warm air. Irritated by all the noise and violence, the fly had been humming angrily about the speckled ceiling. Now, seeing all motion ceased, it landed delicately on the broken edge of the clotted thread of blood and began to feed.

Grunting with the effort, Marreq drove the twisted point of the corkscrew hard into Maillot's ear, tearing the outer flesh, then puncturing the eardrum. There was a soft crunch as the tiny bones of the inner ear were destroyed, then grating as it caught on the thicker bone of the skull. The inspector screamed thinly, with the agony and with the shock, and tried to roll his head away.

Standish had managed to get his own head clear and he held on to Maillot, preventing any movement. Throwing his weight on the handle of the corkscrew, Marreq managed to finally force it through the barrier and into the brain. For good measure he gave it a couple of turns, tangling and crushing the strands of the brain.

That done, he stood up, leaving the handle protruding like some monstrous hearing-aid. 'You may let him go now. I think he is no longer a threat.'

The body still threshed and rolled. The eyes opened and closed and the fingers grasped and scrabbled. Standish let go and also stood up, watching the death throes with dispassionate interest. The wrecked nerve ends gradually ceased to function, as the impulses faded away. The right hand suddenly flung out and down, slapping at the lino. The fly, still busy feeding, was caught by surprise and splattered to nothing in the sticky pool of blood.

The last breath in Mallot's lungs was released in a rattling groan, and he was dead.

'You took your bloody time, Jean. That fascist bastard knew savate and he nearly did for me.'

Marreq grinned. It was rare that Standish betrayed his feelings to that extent and it amused the little apache. 'My most profound apologies, Lord Standish. Sadly, this offal was cunning enough to lock the front door behind him, and there were some unpleasant railings to be negotiated before I could render you any assistance.'

The gun still lay under the bed, and Standish picked it up. 'See, Jean. He even used a Gestapo hand-gun. A Mauser. I'll take it with me; it might come in useful in Poland. That reminds me, while you were enjoying the late lamented lady there, I got us tickets on the night sleeper to Amsterdam. Van der Helde has used his contacts with the Dutch Nazi Party to get us on a boat into Danzig. The crew have been told that we're spies who have to get back into Germany by the back door. Johann has let slip that we've got information about a British invasion of Russia from the north, so his Polish friends will speed us on our way, and keep their mouths shut.'

'When will we be in Warsaw?'

Standish thought for a moment. 'We should be in Danzig on Wednesday evening. If Zbigniev has done his stuff, he should have us holed up safe in Warsaw by mid-day on Thursday. That'll fit in nicely with what I promised Tristram.'

Marreq nodded, then looked about the claustrophobic little room, wrinkling his nose at the heavy smell of double death. 'What are we going to do here? Just leave it? The Blessed Virgin herself knows what the brains at the Quai des Orfèvres will make of this mystery. Who slaughtered who, and why.' He laughed – a giggle rather than a laugh – a sinister sound. 'By then, you and I will be well away.'

'Back to your place, I think. Pick up our papers. Then, on to the Gare du Nord. God Almighty! What on . . . ?' Standish shuddered. 'Jean, do you have to do that?'

'That' was delicately unscrewing the handle of the implement that had killed Maillot, tugging out threads of grey brain, releasing a trickle of bright red blood. With a caper, Marreq got it free and waved it triumphantly in the air.

'Frightfully bad etiquette you know, John. To leave a corkscrew still in like that. Besides, it should give one more problem to the flics. Now, after you. I believe that I can close and lock that window behind us.'

As they walked back through the early evening rush hour, the hunchback tossed the glittering corkscrew in his hand, catching it by the polished handle. Seeing Standish smiling, he asked him why.

'Because, Jean, I'm not sure if we were right to leave the body there. I think a Maillot '40 should be served at room temperature. Not left to chill.'

CHAPTER FOUR

A little of the right money at the right time, hidden by an appeal to his loyalty to the Reich, persuaded the captain of the Motor Vessel *Lipiec* to 'lose' one of his dinghies over-board when he was only a mile or so off Gdynia – less than twenty miles from Danzig.

There had been no trouble at Amsterdam. Johann van der Helde – leading member of the Dutch Nazi Party, ex-mail robber, farmer and valuable unit in 'The Killers' – had arranged the passage and the papers. Then he had returned, without meeting them, to his white house near Arnhem, where he found windows broken and swastikas daubed on doors. Slogans accused him of being a lover of Hitler. One of his cows had been painted with yellow stars and then shot.

He shrugged philosophically, and began to clear up.

The fog had been thick on the Baltic, as it so often was in March. So progress had been slow. Which was something of a relief for Marreq, who had been throwing up in the scuppers for most of the first part of the journey. They had rowed in quietly through the sea-wrack, and left the boat outside the harbour, upside-down, to aid the captain's story of its being lost.

It wasn't difficult to steal two bicycles, and they were in Danzig before dawn. There were a number of German and Polish patrols about, strolling in pairs or in groups, with their Lugers in unbuttoned holsters on their belts. Most notices were in both Polish and German, and pictures of Hitler were prominently displayed everywhere.

There was still two hours to wait, and they spent much of it walking among the shoppers round the main square. A cup of dreadful ersatz coffee from a stall helped to warm them up, but Standish wasn't prepared to risk trying to get a meal.

Although Marreq was a man of a great many virtues, the ability to blend into a crowd wasn't one of them. His hunched back and slight build attracted too many glances for their peace of mind. It was a great relief when noon came and they were able to make their way to the concourse of the old railway station.

'Boli mnie w prawym ramieniu.'

It took a lot to shock John Standish, but to be suddenly told, in the middle of a German-held city, by a most lovely girl, that she had a pain in her right arm – without any other kind of conversational opening – was too much. He just stood there and gaped.

Still speaking in Polish, the girl tried again. 'Pan Standish; do you not recognize me? Have I changed that much?'

'Anna! What on earth was all that nonsense about having a bad arm?'

Her teeth shining, she smiled at his bewilderment. 'Since we are conspirators, I thought we should have some unlikely password.' The smile vanished. 'Please don't tell my father. He takes all this so seriously.'

Standish took her arm and walked her towards the large board showing departures and arrivals. Though he appeared to be smiling and holding her arm gently, his fingers gripped like pincers and his voice was low and harsh. 'In the last week, two men and a girl, only a little older than you, have died because this operation is important. We are here to get a man out of the hands of the Gestapo. It isn't some schoolgirl's game. It *is* serious. I am very tempted to tell Zbigniev, so that he can try and hammer in some sense about who we are and what we are doing.'

The girl looked suitably chastened. Her head hung forward, the silky black hair slipping across her face, masking her clear, blue eyes.

'I am sorry. I wanted to show you that I was no longer a

scared little child, and that a big operation doesn't scare me. So, I made the joke. Believe me, I know how serious it is, this game we play.'

Standish finally relented and smiled. 'I remember when I saw you last, you made a smoke bomb and put it down your privy; it went off at a profoundly embarrassing moment.'

They walked slowly across the city, towards the station, Marreq a few paces at the rear. Anna giggled at the memory. 'Uncle John, do you remember what you did?'

'Perfectly. I caught you. Pulled down your knickers – navy-blue if I remember – and spanked your bottom till it was as red as a turkey's wattles. And, young lady, you are old enough to call me "John". The word "Uncle" always makes me feel damnably old. But, you aren't too old not to let me take your pants down again, if the occasion warrants it. So, be careful.'

She put her arm through his, letting her fingers brush at the palm of his hand. 'John, I am grown up. If you were to take my knickers off now, it might have a different result from last time.' With a laugh, she pulled away and ran a few paces.

Standish also laughed. 'You little minx. You know, you look like your mother when you laugh like that.' He turned to the Frenchman just behind them and said in a low voice. 'It's true, Jean. Little Anna is quite a big girl now.'

Marreq spat in the gutter. 'I would think a little care might be exercised. From what I remember of Zbigniev, he might not take kindly to any lecherous man, even an English milord, inserting his carving knife into that particular piece of white meat.'

Anna took them both to a quiet café and handed over the false papers. Since the country had been partitioned by the Germans and the Russians, it was impossible to know from outside how and when the papers and identity cards were being changed.

First there was the normal identity card that all Poles had to carry at all times. Then there were the work permits; it had been fixed that these would show Marreq and Standish were skilled carpenters who had been working in the shipyards at Danzig.

Their travel permits were overstamped by the Bahnschutzpolizei – the German railway police. Anna had used the excuse that she needed to visit an aunt in Danzig – a perfectly genuine relative – and she had more papers overstamped by the officials of the Befehlshaber der Ordungspolizei – the special uniformed police in countries occupied by the Axis powers.

'It's lucky you didn't wait another week. They say that we'll need *another* of these rotten bits of cardboard. The Sicherheitspolizei und des Sicherheitsdientes – they're sort of spies without uniforms, and a lot of them are Poles who've betrayed the mother country – are going to issue permits as well. Anyway, here's all your stuff. Tickets – third class – and here's a safe address in case you can't make it to our place. Watch out for Nazis on the train. They're getting more suspicious these days.' She raised her chipped cup of brown coffee to drink a mock toast to their success. She had barely opened her mouth when she felt a painful blow on the ankle.

Leaning forwards, Standish spoke softly. 'Anna. I would ask that you remember the worlds of Lobkowitz. He said: "When the tiger has eaten and is sleeping, the elephant may pass in safety. But, when the tiger is hunting, let the butterfly beware how he alights on a leaf." Do you understand?'

Marreq spoke: 'In other words, my vision of quite apocalyptic beauty. Keep your damned mouth shut!'

The journey to Warsaw by rail was long and tedious. The train was old, and the crowded carriages stank of sweat, urine and potted meats. The benches in the third class had only leaking horsehair cushions, and the windows remained obstinately closed despite the stuffiness. Since Marreq had the most rudimentary Polish, it was agreed that he would either sleep, or pretend to sleep, for as much of the journey as possible.

Watching the dreary landscape drag by through the dirty

glass, Standish felt himself slipping away into sleep. Anna had felt it safer to stay in another compartment, so that there would be no way that she could be linked to them. They had been checked twice by railway police. Finally, when they had been travelling for over four hours, Standish fell asleep.

He was woken up by a brutal kick on his shins by a highly-polished jackboot. A stern voice was asking him – for what was obviously not the first time – for his papers. Standish muttered a hasty 'Slucham?', only to be met by a clout across the face with the German officer's gloved hand.

He fumbled in his pockets and produced the papers, hoping that they were good enough to stand up to a German surprise check. This was no cursory examination. The train had been delayed earlier, and there had been talk of action by a group of Polish activists. A derailment! Or, so someone had said.

The cold grey eyes peered at him from under the high peak of the cap. Comparing the face with the picture. No words. No apologies for the blow. The Master Race never apologized to its subjects. A nod of the head, and the papers were thrown back at him.

'Dziekuje,' he muttered, hoping that the thanks wouldn't be taken as sarcasm.

He risked a quick glance out of the window, and was surprised to see a vast, yellow river, rolling beneath the train. The Vistula. That meant he'd been asleep for longer than he'd guessed. Warsaw must only be a matter of minutes away.

The hollow note of the wheels changed. They were off the bridge, and gaining speed. In the far corner, he saw to his horror that the other German officer was trying to question Marreq in bad Polish.

Leaning forward, Standish coughed respectfully to attract the German's attention. He pointed at Marreq and said: 'Ucho. Gluchy.' Then, as though racking his brains for the right German word, he said: 'Stumm.' At last it got through to the officers that the hunchback was a deaf-mute. With a shrug of the shoulders, they gave him back his papers and left the compartment, slamming the door shut.

The two 'killers' exchanged glances. It had been a tricky moment.

None of the other Poles in the carriage had looked at them while the Germans were there, but now they had gone, everyone was all smiles.

Ostentatiously, Marreq stretched and walked out into the corridor. He had used the curved finger sign to Standish, meaning that he needed to talk to him urgently.

When he joined him, in the swaying passage between the carriages, Marreq was looking worried. 'My seat is next to the corridor and I watched those fucking Kraut shits after they left. I fear me that our little charade didn't quite succeed in fooling them. I watched them, and they were talking to one of those ridiculous old men who pretend to be railway police. They pointed our way, and one of the Germans ...'

'What?'

Marreq glanced away at the darkening plain outside Warsaw. When he spoke again, he didn't look at Standish. 'He was holding up his shoulder. Pretending that he was like I am. I know it could have been a ... a joke. But, it didn't seem that way. I beg you to believe, John, that I can tell when I am being mocked. Those Germans weren't mocking me. They were describing me.'

Their talk was interrupted by the sliding door at the other end of the carriage being thrown back. Above the rattle of the wheels, they could hear the clicking sound that one quickly recognizes. The noise made by the heels of jackboots.

'Wait here. I'll be in the toilet.' There was no time for more talk. The officers were nearly on them. A short way behind them, Standish could just hear the shuffling of the worn boots of the Polish guard. An old man with silver Franz Joseph moustaches.

God be praised, the toilet wasn't occupied. He slid the polished door closed and put across the sign with the single word 'Zajety'. Pressing his ear to the door, he waited. Some men might have cursed that they had left the Mauser automatic in the baggage. That would have been a futile and time-wasting exercise. Standish reached under his left arm and drew his leaf-bladed throwing knife out of the soft chamois leather pouch. Both edges were honed to a lethal sharpness.

He was as ready as he could be. All he was able to do now was wait and see how the cards were delivered on the table. Then, he could decide how to play them.

Marreq involved himself in peering through the window of the train, pretending not to notice the approaching Germans. Only when one pushed him hard on the shoulder did he turn round, a look of innocent surprise on his face. The taller of the Nazis, his face tugged down by a puckered scar under the right eye, had his hand resting nervously on the butt of his Luger Parabellum. He asked to see Marreq's papers again, and the hunchback feigned bewilderment. 'Your papers, you ignorant little lump of pig-shit!' bellowed the officer.

Silently, Standish eased back the bolt, opening the door a fractional space, his eye instantly taking in the scene and the placing of the main actors. Jean faced him, his eyes not betraying for a second that he had seen the door move. Both Germans had their back to the toilet, and the elderly Polish guard was leaning against the side of the corridor, only his shoulder visible. The shorter German also had his holster unbuttoned, but his hand was hooked into the broad leather belt.

Fumbling in his pocket, Marreq finally produced the tattered bunch of papers and held them out, twisting his face into an ingratiating leer. Just as the tall German reached out to take them, there seemed to be a sudden lurch of the train, throwing the hunchback forward against him. At the same time, the door of the toilet swung open and Standish was out in a blur of violent movement.

His left hand grabbed at the high collar of the shorter officer, while the knife in his right hand slashed at the exposed jugular vein. Blood jetted out in a bright spray, splattering the walls of the train. Before the first drops of blood had reached the dusty floor, Standish had dropped the knife and grabbed at the Luger. Letting the falling weight of the German help him tug it out. His thumb slipped easily to the safety catch, nudging it off. The dying man flailed backwards at him, and he pushed out savagely with his knee to shove him down the corridor, away from the action.

Standish caught a glimpse of the guard, his mouth open in a parody of extreme shock. Blood spotted across his face, masking his eye. No sound came from him, but his lips moved and strained for a scream. Oddly, the man who sprawled dying had made no great protest at such a savage ending to his life, moaning once, then lying still.

Feeling the cold steel rough against his right palm, Standish used his left hand to pull back on the toggle action of the automatic, cocking it. The brass-jacketed bullet now lay snugly in the breech, ready for the spring to release the firing pin and detonate the explosive.

Marreq and the other German still grappled clumsily in the corner. The Nazi cursing under his breath as he tried to reach his own gun. The hunchback had wrapped his arms about his body, making movement difficult.

It's doubtful if the officer even knew what was happening. The scuffle had been brief, and the sound of the train rattling over an uneven set of points had drowned the noise of the gun being cocked.

Without any warning, the train roared into a tunnel and everything became black. Its whistle screeched like a banshee over a lonely moor, and the vibration increased. Standish was thrown back against the guard, treading heavily on the corpse of the German as he did so. The old man was shaking like a willow in a thunderstorm, and babbling to himself, to Standish, to his God, to anyone. 'Please sir, my pension, not me, blood, better clean it, pension, not me, old man, fought the Russians, please sir. I'll lose my pension.'

His feeble hands grabbed at Standish, hanging on like a suffocating man. Tension pulling his lips back off the teeth,

Standish crashed the gun into his mouth, or where he reckoned his mouth must be. The fingers relaxed.

Although it was getting dark, the burst of light as the train came from the tunnel was stunning. It revealed a scene from some macabre and cramped corner of Hell. Down the corridor, a middle-aged woman stood, teetering on the near edge of a piercing scream, holding a small boy by the hand. The guard, half-sat, half-lay across the narrow space, blood staining his silver moustache, spitting out bits of broken denture. His legs were across the leather-coated body of the short German, who was stretched out as loose as a long-drowned corpse, the face rolling stickily in a spreading pool of bright arterial blood.

In the corner, the tall Nazi had managed to get his gun out and cock it. Fighting for balance, he was trying to wrench the barrel away from Marreq's fingers so that he could get in a clear shot. His gloves and heavy coat also handicapped him. But, he was much the bigger and stronger man and the space gave no opportunity for Marreq to use any of his apache tricks.

Steadying himself against the toilet door, Standish placed the barrel of his Luger against the small of the man's back, angled slightly away from Jean – a bullet from a Luger Parabellum fired at such a range will almost certainly go clean through the body of even the most solidly built men and could well kill anyone too close on the other side – and squeezed the trigger.

The report was crashingly loud in the confined area, and it touched off the woman's scream. Because the gun was pressed so hard against the Nazi's back, there was little recoil and no smoke. The nine millimetre bullet left the barrel at a speed of one thousand and fifty feet per second, tearing through the successive layers of leather, uniform jacket, cotton shirt, woolen vest, skin, flesh, kidneys, stomach, then out again through the reverse order. Though the velocity had been considerably slowed, and the soft lead had been squashed and distorted, there was still enough power for it to richochet from the metal window fitting and spin unevenly down the corridor, clipping the stone neatly out of a ring on the woman's finger.

The impact threw the German forward into the tight embrace of Marreq, his mouth opening wide in surprise. His fingers clutched the trigger and the bullet smashed into the train's roof. His head came back and the cap, with its gleaming peak, dropped off at Standish's feet. Marreq pushed him back, so that he fell across the body of his comrade. He struggled against the massive internal injuries to sit up, fumbling at the gun, trying to cock it and fire again. Failing, he managed to raise it, so that it pointed waveringly in the direction of Standish.

The German's mouth opened, dark blood trickling from the corners. He coughed once, then became firm in his intention. Again, his finger whitened on the trigger. 'Bang!', he said.

And died.

More people poured out into the corridor, shaken by the explosions and screams. Among them was a German infantryman, trying to get his rifle – the Mauser KAR 98K – unslung among the weaving mob of Poles.

'Time to get off. Open the door, quick, Jean.'

But, the door was old and had expanded in the warm weather. Marreq had to smash the window in with the butt of the other Luger before he could reach through and twist the handle from outside. Standish stooped and picked up his beloved throwing knife, stowing it away in its sheath.

A scant twenty paces away, the stormtrooper had managed to beat the crowd away long enough to get his rifle off his shoulder. Yelling hysterically in German at the Poles to get out of his way, it would be only seconds before he opened fire.

Cocking the Luger, Standish aimed carefully over the heads of the crowd in the classic pistol-shooting position. Left arm straight down the side, hand poised on the crest of the hipbone. Pistol held out at the end of an extended right arm. Body pivoted slightly, both eyes open. Gently, squeeze the trigger.

'Bloody good shooting, John. Ninety-eight. That one that wandered must have been the first. Didn't allow for the wind up here on the butts. Stronger than you'd think. Thing that amazes me, John, is why you shoot so bloody fast. No need you know. Take the time and you'd be doing consistently higher scores. There's not a bloody Pathan bearing down on you waving a bloodstained kris, with a gang of his mates alongside.'

'True, Peter. But, you never know when there might be.'

The bullet hit the soldier in the right cheek, the aim spoiled by the swaying of the train. The next shot blossomed darkly at the centre of the man's forehead, like a crimson spider dropped from the ceiling.

Standish waited only for the second necessary to spot the result of his snapshooting, then moved to the open door. The train was rattling along the top of an embankment, the fields below shrouded in the gathering gloom. There were no telegraph poles or fence, as far as they could see.

The door swung crazily in the buffeting wind, making talk difficult. Standish put his mouth to Jean's ear and bellowed. 'You first! Wait! I'll find you! Go!!!'

The frail figure vanished, whipped out of sight by the slipstream. Instantly, Standish followed him, enjoying for a half second the exhilaration he always felt when leaping from a plane. Instinctively, he tucked up his knees and rolled the moment he hit the ground. As the embankment dropped steeply, he was able to roll all the way down, gasping with pain as his shoulder hit something hard. Then he was still, lying on his back in what smelled like clover, watching the lights of the train snaking away above and beyond him.

He stood up, feeling first for the gun tucked into his belt, then for the knife under his arm. The papers were still in his wallet, bulking out the inside pocket of his stained jacket. Not far away to the south and east, he could see the glow in the sky that must be the smelting works on the edge of Warsaw.

His eyes were already getting accustomed to the darkness,

and he began to trot at a steady pace towards where he knew Marreq would be.

He found the Frenchman sitting comfortably on the grass, taking a quick drag from a dented flask of brandy. Standish took it off him and drank, feeling the alcohol burn away some of the tension.

'Come on Jean. Still a lot of walking to do. They'll soon have men out, and we want to be in the city before then. And before they put on the curfew.'

Marreq stood up, stretching his body, feeling his arms and legs to make sure that no bones were broken.

'I was always under the foolish impression that the least comfortable journey in the world was between Concorde and Madeleine on a Friday evening. Now, I know different.'

They set off along the side of the railway. Standish leading at a good pace. He suddenly stopped and looked up at a large white sign, with bold black letters, easily visible even in the dusk. He laughed, saying: 'My God, Jean. As if we weren't in enough trouble. They catch us now and they'll really throw away the key.'

'Why, what does that say?'

'Obcym wstep wzbroniony.'

'And what the hell does that mean?'

'Trespassers will be prosecuted!'

CHAPTER FIVE

'Pan Standish, it is an honour to have you and Pan Marreq in my house once again. I am only sorry that these are such dark times for the entertaining of friends.'

John Standish clasped the hand of the man before him and looked him over, measuring the toll taken by the last few years. Remembering times past.

Zbigniev Cybultna. By far the oldest of the members of 'The Killers' – nearly sixty – with two sons who had fought against the Russo–German alliance. And one daughter; Anna, now aged twenty and a most beautiful girl, with the classical high cheeks and fine complexion of Polish women.

Standish noted with concern the grey skin and tired eyes of his old friend. Life had obviously not been kind under the Occupation. His garage still functioned, though parts had become increasingly hard to come by. Yet, people were still loyal to the memory of a man who had once been one of Poland's greatest racing drivers. Although past his best, Cybultna had taken on the top in Europe – Nuvolari, Carracciola and the darkly handsome Englishman, Dick Seaman – and beaten them.

'John, you are thinking I now look an old man. No, you know me better than to have to lie to me. I had a disagreement with some of the house-painter's bully-boys down on Grochowska Street, and my head proved to be a little softer than their rifle butts. I haven't been the same since then.'

Standish looked around the neat apartment. He noticed the picture of the two boys – Andrzej and Jerzy – smiling sheepishly for a photographer, in their new battle-dresses. He pointed to it. 'Where are they now? Eating their heads off in some prisoner-of-war camp, I suppose?'

The joke was met with a dull silence. Zbigniev turned and walked out of the room, not even bothering to make a polite excuse. Anna moved to the small cupboard in the corner and knelt down, taking out the bottle of Polish vodka. Without a word, she poured out a small glass for Marreq and Standish.

Draining the fiery liquid in one draught, Standish spoke quietly. 'Anna. What did I say about Andrzej and Jerzy? I heard that they'd been taken prisoner by the Russians, somewhere near Smolensk. What's happened?'

The girl sat down in one of the deep armchairs, her eyes on her glass. 'We don't know. Papa had an official form from the Germans saying that they had been captured and were being held by the Russians. Then we got a sort of standard letter from Andrzej, just saying that they were both well, though Jerzy had a knee injury. That they were in a camp in the east with about eight thousand other officers.'

Getting up to pour himself another drink, Marreq tried to cheer her. 'Anna, I don't see why that should make you so miserable. They are at least safe and warm. The Russians are hardly likely to murder that number of men. The outrage would be terrible.'

She looked up, her eyes brimming with tears. 'Suppose it was done secretly. Oh, I don't know.' And she began to weep in earnest.

Unnoticed, Zbigniev had come back into the room. 'It is well that you should shed tears for your murdered brothers, Anna. And for all Polish young men.'

Gently, Standish interrupted him. 'Zbigniev, how can you know?'

'I have a friend; he used to be my mechanic before the War. He lives near the forest of Katyn, about twelve miles west of Smolensk. A week ago he came here, risking his life to travel from the Russian zone. In March, he had been poaching in the woods. He heard lorries coming so he hid in the undergrowth to see what was happening. There were many lorries, all guarded by the Russians. Out of them, came Poles. All officers.

My friend could see that most had their hands bound behind them, some with hemp and some with baling wire. Soldiers, armed with automatic weapons, guarded them closely. A few made a run for it and they were shot down.'

His voice broke and he walked to the window, looking out at the blackness. 'They were murdered. All of them. Thrown into pits and the earth dragged over them by tractors. My friend saw lime poured on top. Hundreds of young men. He ran away that night and didn't go back for weeks. He found mass graves. Big enough for twenty thousand men. From their uniforms, he knew what units they were from, and which camps they had been in. I ask you to believe that I know my sons were there and were slaughtered. John, they were only nineteen and twenty-one. Boys.'

There was nothing to be said. The old man went to bed early and Anna told them more about the massacre at Katyn. Though some Poles had heard the dreadful rumours, German and Russian censorship was too tight for news to spread. And, anyway, who would believe such a dreadful tale? The Germans cast their net of terror wide. A cousin of Anna had been taken from his bed at Sroda and marched through the streets with twenty of his friends in September of the previous year. A gang of Schutz Staffel soldiers had made them dig graves with their bare hands, then lined them up and made them shout "Heil Hitler". Then the S.S. had shot them down. Burying the wounded alive. It was animals like that who held Poland in their grip.

It was the Gestapo who held Leslie Peters in their cells in the anonymous building on Belwederska Street, overlooking Lazienki Park. With twenty other suspected members of the Warsaw underground.

'Wouldn't they have tortured them by now? They've held them for a couple of weeks.'

'They believe in softening them up by lack of food and sleep. They will all have had a preliminary investigation, but none of them would have cracked. The serious stuff starts any day now.'

'So, we must move fast. I suppose we are lucky that the Gestapo don't realize what a catch they've made. They could have taken the whole bunch to their headquarters and we'd never have got them out.'

'What would you have done?'

It was Marreq who answered her. 'We hope, with the aid of your father, to remove these prisoners alive. If that proves impossible, then we will, with the utmost regret, have to try and kill them all. This man Peters knows much. Far too much. So we would have to try and silence him. All we could do would be to try and ensure that as many as possible of the enemy were sent to their Nazi Valhalla at the same time. Now, if you will please excuse me, Mademoiselle, the day has been a little more arduous than I like. I would like to retire to my bed. Perhaps an omelette first? If that is not putting you to a lot of trouble.'

She looked embarrassed. 'I'm sorry Pan Marreq. Eggs are not available unless you have influential friends on the Black Market.'

Marreq looked pensive for a moment. 'Perhaps there might be something I can do to help. I have a comrade or two in this lovely city. In the meantime, I shall go to my sleep hungry. It's yet another score to chalk up against that Austrian Corporal Schicklegruber. Goodnight, my child. John, Zbigniev. Goodnight.'

The next day they held a planning meeting. Apart from Standish and Marreq, Zbigniev had brought along three other members of the underground. A skinny musician named Jan Loza. A chubby butcher – Tadeusz Janczar. And a soldier who moved from safe house to safe house, constantly on the move. He was known as 'Major', and nothing else. He had only one eye.

Standish and Marreq learned how the group had been picked up. Apparently a random swoop by the Gestapo. About the layout of the old hotel on Belwederska Street, with its kitchens converted to dungeons. Janczar had used to deliver meat there before the War and was able to help a lot.

Summing-up, Standish raised one problem. 'We're agreed then that only ten men can pull it off. You've got the guns. But, to blow our way in there, we'll need explosive. Who can get that?' He looked sideways at Cybultna, who got up and excused himself. 'Yes, I think I'll have to go for a leak as well. Won't be a minute.'

In the other room, as he'd expected, he found Zbigniev waiting for him. 'I have some, John. You know that, when Maria knew she was dying, she made me promise to give up safe-blowing, and I was just getting ready for a big job. I kept my promise. It's up in the loft. Carefully wrapped. Every now and again I take it down, and long to use it on the Nazis.'

'Well. Now's your chance. How long before we move?'

The old man pondered. 'It will take a day to get every detail organized. The earliest would be Saturday evening. But, the guard is bound to be that bit slacker on the Sunday. I think that one in the afternoon – that's when they change duties for lunch – would be best. I can arrange the transport; I'll get a lorry and a couple of cars. I'll drive the lorry. Don't look so worried my son. I may be old and look a bit decrepit, but you will find no better driver in Warsaw. Except possibly Anna. She's inherited all my cunning with motor vehicles. She may even be that tiny space better than I at tuning engines. I'll arrange to have them stolen and tuned tomorrow.'

Saturday was a quiet day. Standish spent it largely in sleeping, staying in bed till midday. Then he was interrupted by Anna. 'John! Quick, get up!'

Throwing on one of her father's dressing gowns, he strode out into the living-room. There, his face a mask of worry, was the plump figure of the butcher, Tadeusz Janczar. In his hands he held two large sheets of paper.

'Now, Anna, what's all the fuss? Hey, where's Marreq

gone? Is he in the bathroom?'

Her hands clasping nervously at each other, Anna answered him. 'Pan Marreq said that he hated being cooped up in one room. He said something about it reminding him of the time he was locked in a small cage by the Imperial Dragon Tong with only eighty lepers for company. A tong is a Chinese gang, isn't it? Anyway, he was out by seven, saying he had some friends who would help him find somewhere else to stay. So that we wouldn't be so crowded here. I wanted to wake you, but he said not to worry you and that you'd understand. Do you understand, John?'

Standish gnawed angrily at his lip. 'Yes. Bloody hell! I understand. What he said about the lepers. It wasn't a joke; it really happened to him, when the tong wanted to persuade him to kill a merchant in Sungchow for them. The merchant happened to be a friend. In the end, they pointed out that if force wouldn't make him do it, would he remember that they had paid him as an assassin. To save you asking, he killed the man they wanted. Then left the country. Jean has odd ideas of honour. Ever since then he hasn't been able to stand inaction or being closed up.'

The butcher wiped sweat from his face. 'But, where can he have gone?'

'Don't worry.' Standish laughed. 'Jean Marreq will have friends in every city and town in the world. Wherever the underworld gathers in the darkness, there will be someone there who knows Jean Marreq. Nobody knows him here who would betray him to the Germans. And, the Germans won't have heard of him. Not yet. He's safe.'

Tadeusz threw the papers on the table. 'You think so. I doubt if he is still at liberty. Not after this. We are all in danger.'

Hiding his concern, the Englishman strolled to the table and flipped over the top sheet. It was a crudely printed poster, the heavy ink still wet. In both German and Polish, it offered a substantial reward for information on a man involved in the murder of three German soldiers on the Danzig train, just outside Warsaw on the previous day. 'Tall and slender, wearing a light brown tweed jacket.'

'Christ, is that all you were worried about? That could fit half the men in Poland. Well, several thousand anyway.'

Anna herself turned over the other poster. The heading was the same. A reward from the headquarters of the Warsaw Geheime Staatspolizei for the assassin from the train killings. It was signed over the stamp of the Protector of the 'General Government' – the infamous Hans Frank.

He didn't need Anna's finger, shaking slightly with the tension, to point out to him the passage in the middle of the poster, under the heading: 'Description.'

'This outlaw can be easily recognized by any citizen, and all Poles are encourged to be on the look-out for him. From the cowardly manner of the killings of loyal German soldiers, whose only function was to aid and protect the liberated peoples of Poland, it is obvious that this man is dangerous. No attempt should be made to apprehend him, but he should be followed and reported to the appropriate authorities. He acts as a deaf-mute, but he is believed to be of foreign extraction. Well below average height. He is notably a cripple. The brigand is a hunchback.'

'Christ! Now that has torn it. I didn't think they'd get a poster out this fast. And I hoped the silly bugger wouldn't go swanning all over the city.'

As the three of them stared at each other, they were interrupted.

There was a thunderous knocking at the door and a voice shouted; 'Mac hauf! Schnell! Open this door!'

CHAPTER SIX

'Mac hauf! Schnell! Open this door!'

For a moment, Standish thought that Anna was going to faint. Tadeusz crumpled up the posters and looked desperately around for somwhere to hide them. There was another bang on the door and Anna seized Standish by the arm.

'In the loft! There are two water-tanks. The smaller one is a dummy. Quickly!'

'In the name of the German people. Open this door! In the name of that great cock-sucker Adolf Hitler, open the door! Come on John. I'll drop everything.'

'Marreq!' Standish crossed to the door and unlocked it. There stood Jean, grinning all over his creased face, holding a large brown paper bag, stuffed with smaller white paper bags.

'Jean. You stupid cunt! Excuse my language, Anna.'

She smiled. Her voice still tremulous, she spoke to Standish. 'Don't worry, John. I'm old enough to know what the word means, and cross enough to want to use it myself.'

Putting down his parcels, Marreq started to unpack. 'Huh. There's gratitude. I bring you three dozen, not two dozen, mind, but three dozen, eggs. I bring you sugar. White sugar. Tea and coffee. Not bloody ground-up acorns ravaged from some innocent oak-tree. Coffee. And golden butter, tasting of sunlight and rolling green meadows. And more. So, please forgive my ill-conceived jest and let us have something to eat that doesn't taste as though it was reconstituted cardboard and dog's puke. No slur is intended on your cooking, my dear Anna. In fact, it . . . ' He was suddenly aware of the chill that still hung in the flat.

'Look at this, Jean. They've got your number.'

The hunchback picked up the poster, and peered at it. Hesitating over some of the phrases that weren't familiar to him. Then, he threw it down. 'So? It could be anybody with a ricked back.'

Standish rolled his head in disbelief. 'No, Jean. It's the end for you. There just aren't that many . . . who fit that description in Warsaw. Or in the whole of Poland. See sense. There's a good chap.'

Marreq turned savagely on him. 'Oh. "There's a good chap." Who the hell do you take me for, you damned English bastard? I've told you before, John, I cannot tolerate any man patronizing me. I've made a few contacts with the Market. That's where I was able to locate one or two essential edibles and comestibles. For a small outlay, and the promise of more, I've set up in a flat of my own for the next couple of days, up on Stoleczna Street, near the Fortress. I can come and go, be drunk or sober, with no man any the wiser.'

Anna interrupted him. 'Please, Pan Marreq. The Germans have this city totally under their control. If you venture out, then they will find you and hunt you down. Through you they may reach others.'

With studied calm, Standish turned his back. 'She's right, Jean. I'm sorry after coming all this way and after what has happened so far. But, you will have to get out of the city as soon as possible. Get back to Paris, and we'll meet up with you at your place down in St. Germain-des-Prés. We'll fix up the details with Zbigniev when he gets back.'

'No.'

'What?'

'I said "No", and that's what I mean. I came here to help you on a mission and that's what I'll do. Nobody, even you, John, will tell me where I am to walk and how I am to carry myself and when I must come and go. No!'

Anna touched the gaping Tadeusz on the arm, and they both went into the other room, closing the door behind them. The two members of 'The Killers' faced each other across the table.

'Jean, is there nothing that I can say to make you see reason?'

Marreq grinned and sat down. 'You could kill me. Or, I think it might be more strictly accurate to say that you are at liberty to attempt to kill me.'

Standish grinned back. 'I recall the words of the mighty Lobkowitz, who said: "When the lion braves the tiger, then the jackal and the scorpion rejoice." I'm not sure that isn't inflating our importance, but you know what I mean. There is much that I would do to check the Jerries, but killing one of my few close friends isn't one of them. But, be careful, Jean. If I can think of a way of stopping you staying in Warsaw, then I'll use it. Is that a deal?'

'Yes, John. Here's my address and my telephone number. Now I have to go back and cook myself a small quiche. I have a hunger from all my foraging. I'll be in touch tomorrow morning.'

Walking across to open the door for him, Standish felt some comment was called for. 'Tomorrow then. If you're still here.' Marreq passed by and went towards the stairs. Another thought came to him, and he shouted out. 'Jean, thanks for the food.'

The last sound he heard was that sinister giggle, then the hunchback was gone. At the sudden silence, Standish shuddered slightly. 'Someone walking over my grave,' he said to himself. And closed the door.

The flat was quiet and empty. Zbigniev had been out all day, making the plans for the stealing of the transport. Then, he would hold a meeting in a tavern with the other members of the group. He would not be back before midnight. The little butcher was long gone, back to his shop. Anna had also left, to do some shopping and to try and get hold of some grenades and ammunition.

Standish was all alone. On the table in front of him was a detailed street map of Warsaw, with lines drawn on it in different colours. A bottle of slivovitz, half-empty and a glass, half-full, stood in the centre of the map. He had taken off his watch, and that too lay on the table. On the arm of the chair rested the old-fashioned telephone.

Stubbing out a cigarette, he reluctantly picked up the mouthpiece. When the operator answered, he read out a number from a piece of paper on his lap. The phone rang, and rang. Finally, a male voice answered. In bad Polish.

Speaking in perfect German, Standish asked for the person he wanted. There was a delay, then another man came on. Still Standish insisted on one man in particular. The delay stretched to minutes. Then, the voice of the man he wanted.

'Is that Herr Stürmbannführer Neumann?'

The voice that answered was as soft as sleep and as chill as a serpent's kiss. A voice that would strike fear even into the heart of a corpse. 'It is he. Who is it who speaks?'

'You are looking for the hunchback from the train. I know where he is.'

There was no reply, but Standish knew that the Gestapo agent was hanging on, patiently, waiting for him to go on.

'Send your men to forty-seven, Stoleczna Street. He's living there.'

'Why do you tell me this?' The voice was barely curious, as though a speck of dust moving in the air had deviated in some mildly interesting way. 'Is it money, or revenge?'

'It is neither, Herr Stürmbannführer Neumann. The cripple has upset "die Totschläger".'

This time, there was a distinct intake of breath. 'The Killers! You are sure?'

'Quite. Goodbye. Don't let him escape.'

The click as Standish set down the telephone was very loud in the quiet room. He lay back in the chair, looked at his watch, and began to laugh.

The light was fading from the room when Anna came bursting in, to find Standish asleep in the same chair. The bottle of slivovitz was emptier than before.

His eyes opened incuriously at the noisy entrance. 'My dear little Anna. It seems a speciality of yours to come into the room like a hurricane giving birth to a cyclone. What is it this time?'

'I have bad news, Pan Standish.'

'It must be serious if you forget that my name is "John" and not "Pan Standish". What is it?'

Her face pale, Anna told him. 'The Gestapo have raided the apartment of your friend, Jean. They were seen suddenly rolling up from nowhere in their black coats and soft hats. It happened late this afternoon.'

'And Jean?'

'Nobody knows. They were there a long time, but they didn't seem to have anyone with them. Perhaps he managed to slip away.'

'Perhaps.'

'Why do you smile like that, John?'

Standish yawned and rose from the chair, stretching until all his muscles creaked. 'When you went in the other room, Jean and I had a discussion. What you might call a free and frank exchange of views. Mine were somewhat in conflict with his, and he refused to go. I said that I might be able to find a way to make him less of a threat to us. And I did.'

The girl looked at him unbelievingly. 'What did you do?'

He walked to her and looked down into her eyes. 'Listen you naive child. The important thing is the operation to get the agent out of the hands of the Germans before they find out who he is and how much he knows. Jean Marreq would have been invaluable in that operation, but he was spotted on the train and now the whole damned city is going to be on the lookout for him. So, I had to get him out of the way. I have an ... I suppose you would call it an acquaintanceship, with a certain Major Neumann in the Gestapo. So, I rang him up and mentioned an address and hinted at an organization that he has met in the past. That was all.'

A pall of quiet eased down in the room, wrapping them both in it. 'Are you telling me the truth, John?'

Standish nodded. 'And that sleep had its effect. I feel fit for anything. Go and make a drink of that coffee he brought in, please. I'm glad the boys in black got there. No more problems with Marreq now, eh! Come on! Coffee. He had his uses, I must admit.'

Thin-lipped and pale-faced, Anna walked through into the kitchen. There was the chinking sound as she rummaged through the cutlery drawer. For the first time in her life, she was confronted by the reality of total war. She had heard – and seen – Poles murdered by the Nazis. She had driven cars for underground groups in raids and killings. But, this was different. This Englishman had callously betrayed a friend to the mercies of the Gestapo. Just because he seemed to represent a threat. It was too much for her to take in.

Standish nearly didn't bother to look up when she came in from the kitchen holding the coffee in a pot on a tray. But, he did.

Fortunately.

Because that glance gave him the fraction of shrunken time to move. To move when she threw the boiling coffee at him. To move when she followed it up by launching herself at him with a long-bladed steel carving knife in her hand.

He hurled himself backwards, so that the liquid splashed over the bottom of the chair instead of bubbling into his eyes. The upturned chair checked Anna in her leap, and he had time to get to his feet before she came again at him, moaning softly, low in her throat.

He circled away, watching the knife, not her eyes. He had looked there first, and had seen the whites enlarged with shock. Glazed. She held the knife low, he noticed approvingly, like a good professional. Her father had taught her well.

Standish whispered to her, trying to break her out of the daze. 'Anna. Listen to me, love. I rang up Neumann at the Gestapo offices.' He pulled back as she feinted at his face then stabbed for his groin. 'Listen. After I rang the Kraut, I rang up Jean. Gave him just enough time to get out. To show him I wasn't joking. He thought it was damned funny. Said he'd be in Paris by Tuesday. And he will. When he gives his word, he always keeps it. Listen.'

But, the words weren't getting through at all. So it had to be actions instead. Waiting until she was leaning forwards, Standish dropped quickly to his knees and then sprang at her, never more than a foot from the floor. He felt the knife rip at his shoulder; heard Anna scream with pure rage as she realized she had been tricked.

He hit her with his left arm, throwing her over on to her back. There was an entrancing glimpse, which registered with him despite the peril of his position, of stocking tops, of soft thigh and of a scrap of white at the top of her legs.

Later. Now he scrambled up her, digging his knees hard into her, forcing her breath out with a whoosh. The hand with the knife still threatened him, so he clipped her hard on the wrist with the edge of his hand, sending the carving blade arcing into the corner of the room, where it stuck trembling in the wainscoting. She strained up at him with the tendons in her neck standing out with the effort of her hatred. Tried to bite him in the throat.

Using his weight and strength, Standish finally subdued her. Then, holding both her hands with one of his, he sat up on her chest and began to slap her hard across the face. First from the left and then back-handed from the right. After every few blows he would stop and ask her if she was prepared to listen to him.

Her eyes closed, mouth open and trying to scream in between the blows, Anna was locked in her own small world of hatred. Her cheeks reddened and a web of blood spread thinly from her mouth. Each slap was punctuated by Standish's words.

'I ... rang ... Gestapo ... then ... I ... rang ... Marreq ... I ... knew ... he ... would ... get ... away ... I ... rang

... Gestapo ... then ...'

Quite suddenly, she opened her eyes and smiled at him. 'You can stop hitting me, John. I'm all right now.'

Without letting go of her wrists, he sat back, easing the weight from her by relaxing on to his knees. He looked carefully at her face, watching for some sign that she was trying to trick him, but the tenseness was gone, and she was perfectly normal.

On impulse, he stretched forward, until his face was close to her, and whispered in her ear. 'I'm sorry, little one.'

Tears gathered in her eyes and her voice was husky when she answered. 'Don't be sorry, John. That would hurt me more than all those slaps.'

And she moved her face to him, and kissed him gently on the lips. He responded to her kiss, letting his tongue probe slowly between her lips, pushing insistently. As he lay on top of her, he was conscious of his swelling hardness.

'Darling Anna. You're very beautiful, but I'm much older than you and I've known your father for ...'

She silenced his words with another long, strong kiss. He let go of her hands and stroked her hair. She took his head between her hands. 'Pan Standish, I am no longer a girl whose bottom needs spanking. I know well that you will not be able to find it in your heart to love me more than a little, for these times are not for lovers. You will have to go back to England, and our fight against the Germans will be long and bitter. Who can see the ending? No, don't try and talk to me, John. There may only be this one moment, this short time out of war. Please take it with me. Tomorrow John, we may both die. I would not want to die without having been loved by a man.'

And she wept in her youth.

With no more words between them, Standish carried her gently into his bedroom, where the evening light softened the lines of the cheap furniture. The window was open, and the warm air carried in the muted sounds of the city.

They undressed each other like lovers who had known each other for many years, touching and kissing each other's bodies. Naked, they climbed into the cool linen cave of the bed, burrowing deep. Standish caressed her breasts, feeling the nipples firm beneath his lips, making her wriggle by rolling them and nibbling them with his teeth. She stroked his maleness, brought his hand to touch her body.

As he moved his hand against her, she moaned softly, and became wet with her love. Carefully, now, unconsciously repeating the position when she had tried to kill him, he rolled on top of her. She guided him into her with quivering fingers, crying out once as he penetrated her. Standish controlled the movement, wishing more than he had ever wished that it would be good for her. He held back, feeling her begin to grind her hips against him, feeling the fluttering of her thighs and stomach.

Then he relaxed, driving himself with her, so that her final jerking shudder brought him to his own sweet climax.

After, he held her close and stroked her hair and whispered quiet words to her. And she cried a little.

'John. I had always wondered what it would be like. I had thought it would be in a fine room after a beautiful wedding, with my strong husband loving me.'

'Are you sorry?'

She pulled away and sat up. 'Oh, John! How can you ask me that? No, no I'm not sorry. It was wonderful. I would not have died without being loved by a man. By a man like you. Thank you, John. Those sound such empty words, but I mean them with all my heart.' Suddenly she was again the efficient Resistance fighter. 'Now I must make some coffee, so that you will be strong for tomorrow.'

She clambered out of bed, speaking as he slapped her affectionately on the bottom. 'Sir, that is no way to treat an innocent maiden. I will tell my father how you deceived me and lured me with your wicked tongue.'

Standish shouted after as she went into the kitchen: 'Beware you young witch. When you return to my lair, I shall show you that my tongue is not only good at deceiving. It also has a fine way with it when it comes to the business of loving.'

He was rewarded with a giggle.

The rattle of a German personnel carrier clattering over the cobbles woke Standish at three the next morning. The plans had all been finalized and everything was ready for the next lunch-time. The vehicles had been stolen and were tuned to the finest pitch by Zbigniev and by Anna. Guns and ammunition were stored in the dummy water tank in their loft.

All that remained was to wait.

He opened the window wider and leaned on the sill, looking over the sleeping city. But, not everyone was sleeping. Somewhere to the west there was the crackle of small arms' fire and a glow in the sky suggested that the partisans had been busy.

Standish lit a cigarette and thought back over the events of the evening. And, he recalled the words of Lobkowitz: 'The War is ceaseless and always with us, as a baying hound at our shoulder. The most that we can look for is an occasional moment of tranquillity in the midst of the conflict.'

CHAPTER SEVEN

Sunday, March 24th, 1940, in Warsaw.

Lunch-time, just after one o'clock. The smell of cooking hung heavy over the city, lingering in the warm air, tugging at your nostrils as you walked the nearly empty streets. Everyone was either sleeping after lunch, eating lunch, or faint with anticipation of a lunch nearly ready.

In less than ten minutes, Unterscharführer Weiss would be able to put his rifle back in the armoury on the second floor, open the tight collar of his uniform and go up to the canteen for his lunch. Two of his friends had just passed him on their way out into the city for an afternoon's relaxation. Pork and sauerkraut, followed by a steamed sponge. A few glasses of good German beer, not the weak piss that the Poles drank, then the rest of the day was his.

He stretched, flexing the muscles in his calves, tight inside the new jackboots. He nodded stiffly at Stürmmann Trepp, as he marched easily round the front of the building, making his slow patrol. Trepp – fucking queer with his Hamburg coarseness. Weiss was an Austrian, like the Führer himself, and felt he was a more cultured man than some of the filth he had to keep his sergeant's eye on.

A hundred yards down Belwederska Street, a small car stopped, and a young girl got out. She began to walk towards him and Weiss straightened up. Although fraternization was against regulations, some of the soldiers managed to sneak out at night for a good time with some of the more amenable local girls. A thought crossed his mind. Only a couple of days ago they'd found one of the Obergefreiters from the other side of the city who'd been seen last with a Polish girl. His throat had been cut. And his penis had been ripped away and stuffed in his mouth.

Maybe he wouldn't bother. The girl was nearer. Good legs. He paced the length of the front steps, noticing as he turned, as he always noticed, the faded patches on the impressive facade where the letters had been taken down. He could have read the name of the Hotel, if he'd been able to read any Polish. It didn't matter, because he'd been told that it used to be the Imperial Hotel, and was once highly rated.

Only a few yards away now, the girl seemed to be hesitating, looking a bit lost. The car that had dropped her was moving again, slowing to let another car overtake it. From the other way, Weiss noticed the clattering of an old lorry, lurching along from the direction of the City Centre.

A slight breeze brought the scent of the lime trees from the large park across the road. It really was a beautiful day to be alive.

Now she was actually coming up to him. He stopped walking and smiled pleasantly at her. Very nice. Lovely eyes and a wave of fine black hair.

'Przepraszam. Jak daleko jest do drogeria?'

What the hell did she want? It looked as though she was asking for directions. She came a little closer, looking forlorn, and a bit frightened at being so close to a German soldier. He racked his brains for the few phrases they were supposed to have memorized. 'Nie sprechen polsku.'

Something like that. She was opening her handbag. To show him what she wanted.

That was what Unterscharführer Johann Weiss thought. He even leaned forward a little, showing his willingness to be of assistance.

It wasn't a bit of paper with directions on it. It was a long, needle-pointed stiletto that Anna pulled out of her bag. And drove up through his throat, angling the blade back as Standish had taught her, so that it penetrated easily through to the base of the brain.

It was done so quickly that Weiss didn't even know what

had happened. He felt a slight prick at his neck, and he began to raise his hand to brush away the insect that had caused it. Then there was a brief moment of red agony somewhere at the centre of his mind. Strangely he was falling, holding at the girl as he slipped down. A gentle, apologetic smile on his face. Perhaps it was the heat. He should explain to this pretty girl.

'Es muss die Hitze sein.'

It seemed as though someone had struck him in the face, then his cheek felt the sun-warmed stone of the pavement. Through dimming eyes he saw feet rushing past him. The sun shone in his face and the pavement seemed bathed in a blood-red glow.

He was dead.

The Poles, led by Standish, ran past the body, while Anna walked quickly to one of the getaway cars. Her father gave a quick wave of the hand from the cab of the old lorry. The explosives were in the hands of the one-eyed Major.

Through the main doors and into what used to be the foyer of the Imperial. The space had been cleared out and only a plain table, with a card marked 'Inquiries' in both German and Polish on it, remained. A handful of soldiers stood about, some armed, some not.

The Poles were armed with both Schmeisser and Bergmann sub-machine guns, spraying the nine millimetre bullets all around. A Gestapo agent, on his way out, was frozen on the grand staircase. A burst from Standish's gun nearly cut him in half, splattering blood and intestines over the marble stairs.

Leaving two men behind to cover the entrance, the rest of the attackers split. Two men went to the head of the stairs to hold them against the main body of soldiers who were known to be on the floors above. A grenade blew out the lift shaft with a spectacular spray of smoke. The cable was severed and two soldiers, escorting a prisoner to the top floor were trapped in it as it fell. All three of them were mangled together.

The main attack went down the stairs to the old kitchens. Here they encountered the first resistance, for no shots had been fired back in the foyer. The Sunday surprise had been total.

Bullets bounced and sang about the narrow corridor at the foot of the stairs.

Standish pulled one of the Poles forward. 'It's a machine gun. Give me a grenade.'

Holding his gun in his left hand, he tugged the pin out with his teeth, counting below his breath. Then he dived out from the bottom of the stairs, hurling the grenade down to his right. The blast threw him back, rolling him against a huge bronze statue of the goddess Athene. His ears ringing, he charged forward, closely followed by the others.

A couple of soldiers lay groaning amidst the tangled wreckage of their gun emplacement. Tadeusz, the butcher, tugged out a long gleaming knife and carefully slit their throats. The groaning stopped. One heavy iron door faced them.

Above, in the foyer, the shooting was becoming fiercer, showing that the opposition was pressing. Time was desperately limited. Standish sent one more man back, then beckoned the Major. Wiping a smear of blood from over his good eye, the Pole clapped three sticks of explosive against the door, and lit a short fuse.

Ducking against the blast, they scuttled back and peered round the corner. Just as the fizzling fuse neared the sticks, the door inched open, and a hand, in a black leather glove, reached round for the explosive. Standish was about to try and shoot at it, when he was brushed aside.

Waving a bayonet in his hand, the thin musician, Jan Loza dashed at the door. 'Come back you bloody fool,' shouted Standish, realizing vaguely the futility of shouting in English as such a moment.

Someone fired from a slit in the iron door, at least one of the bullets grasping at Loza and spinning him to the floor. The door opened a little more, and they could see the edge of the field-grey cuff. The hand had the explosive. Cocked ready to hurl it back at them.

Loza was up again, holding his ruined body together, to move those few yards. He reached the door, clasped the hand, lunging beyond the door with the bayonet. They heard a scream, then more shots. Before they could see the actual moment of Loza's death, the explosive was ignited by the fuse.

The noise was devastating, with pieces of iron flying through the air, whining and biting at the walls and ceiling. When Standish opened his eyes, he found something lying at his foot. It was a hand, and part of a fore-arm. By a freak of the blast, the hand was still wearing a black glove.

Behind the shattered door, the carnage was total. There was not a single German alive. All that stood between them and their target was one more barrier. Flimsier. Steel bars, with one lone soldier, and three civilian jailers. Poles.

The Major spat one word. 'Traitors,' and raised his gun.

Standish pushed the gun down. 'Save time.' Then, to the German. 'Throw down your gun, and open up the door. Now, or I'll order my men to shoot!'

Instantly, the soldier threw down the rifle, and spoke to one of the guards. The man, trembling so much he could hardly get the key in the lock, opened the door. Beyond them, were more doors.

While their prisoners were guarded, one of the Poles took the keys and released all of the victims of the Gestapo. They staggered, or walked, out of their cells, looking at their rescuers with a mixture of bewilderment and disbelief.

Standish took command. 'We have too little time for talk. The men upstairs are holding off vastly superior German forces. Reinforcements are bound to arrive for the Nazis within minutes. I have come from England to rescue a man named Leslie Peters. The rest of you are at liberty to go. But, we cannot help you. You are free, so go now. Where is Peters?'

To his horror, nobody moved. 'For God's sake we'll all get killed. Peters!'

An elderly Pole, his face marked by what looked like cigarette burns, raised a hand. 'We hear you. If what you say is true, we are all in your debt. But, we cannot know that you are not Germans and this is not a trick to get us to betray a man to you. If such a man exists.'

There was a murmur of agreement from the rest of the prisoners. Standish had to admit they had a point. A moment of inspiration came to him. He tugged out his own Luger Parabellum and gave it to the old man who had spoken.

'Those men were your guards? Right; one is an enemy soldier. The others are traitors. Shoot them. Go ahead and shoot them.'

The Pole looked at him disbelievingly, and made no move to raise the gun. Snarling, a younger man at his elbow snatched the gun and put a bullet in the back of the neck of each of the four men lined against the wall. Then grinned and gave the gun back to Standish.

He pointed to a slightly-built man near the back. About thirty, with thinning hair and a receding chin. 'That is the Englishman.'

The man he pointed at came forward, hands casually in his pockets. He nodded to Standish. 'Hello, old boy. Name's Peters. Jolly glad to see you.'

There was an untidy scramble to get out of the dungeon, with freed men fighting each other to be the first out. Which turned out to be a bad idea as the Germans were fighting their way back by some backstairs and had the door at the top of the prison stairs clearly in their line of fire.

The first man out threw his arms wide as the bullets tore into his chest, collapsing dead on top of the others. Firing from the hip, Standish led the counter-charge out into the foyer. Several of the Poles were hit as they battled out of the old hotel, but most made it to the pavement, where Cybultna had the lorry engine revving up ready.

The Major hurled a last packet of explosive back into the building, falling with a bullet through the throat as he completed the throw. But, it was not a wasted sacrifice. Smoke billowed out of the wrecked frontage and there was a lull in the shooting.

Some men broke across the road and ran into the streets in the park. Others headed into the maze of side streets in the direction of the City Centre. But, most climbed into the two cars and the lorry. Suddenly, Standish couldn't find Peters, and he looked about him in desperation. Then he saw him, cowering by the stone lion that guarded the entrance to the Imperial.

'Come on, man!'

Peters scuttled over at the cry, and climbed into the lorry. 'Just waiting for the others to get aboard, old man. That's all.'

The cars were off, heading back on their tracks out of the city. The main German barracks were not that far away, and troops would be flooding in their direction from the middle of Warsaw. Zbigniev glanced at Standish, who hung on the running-board. The Englishman nodded to him, and he let in the clutch and roared off away from the burning Gestapo building.

At the corner of Belwederska Street and Dolna Street, a lone German soldier was returning from an illicit drink. He had heard the shooting and the crump of heavy explosives and had been making his way back to the barracks. He suddenly saw two private cars scream round the corner, and a shot was fired at him. He unslung his rifle, and then saw an old lorry, rattling like a prize collection of scrap iron. A tall, thin figure in torn clothes, with a smoke-darkened face hung on the near-side running-board, waving what looked like a German pistol.

The soldier dropped to his knee and snapped off two shots at the man on the lorry. From his position, he couldn't see whether he hit the man or not, but he guessed he hadn't. He consoled himself by thinking that it was a damned difficult shot anyway.

But it had been well-aimed.

The second bullet hit Standish under the right arm, entering at a slight upwards trajectory, breaking two ribs, narrowly missing the lungs, glancing off a third rib and exiting vertically, snapping the right collar-bone as clean as a blow from an axe.

The impact of the blow knocked him over the side of the cab, dropping him in the lap of one of the freed Poles. Though in a lot of pain, he was still conscious.

'Just keep going. Try and get me to your place. Patch me up. If I'm too bad then ditch me. That's an order.'

Then he passed out.

He came round, lying on the bed in his room at Cybultna's apartment. A face he didn't recognize was bending over him, looking serious. Beyond him, Standish could see the pale face of Anna, and the worried face of Zbigniev. There was no sign of Peters. He moved his head, wincing at the pain, and saw a cloud of cigarette smoke wreathing out of the armchair.

Anna saw his glance and moved to his side. 'Yes, Peters is safe. This is Doctor Powazki. He says that you should be all right but there is internal wounding that could prove fatal if you try and move, for quite a long time.'

Opening his lips was more difficult than he remembered, but he succeeded in framing the words he wanted. 'How long before move?'

It was the doctor who answered him. 'You are very lucky to be alive, Englishman. If you'd been bending over the other way when the bullet hit you, it would have ripped out most of the inside of your chest. As it is ... a few ribs cracked and a collar-bone gone. Those will heal in a couple of weeks. But, I think there may be some internal injuries. There is some bleeding that I cannot trace. If I could get you into my hospital ... but that is out of the question. So, I do not think you can take a chance.' He saw Standish's lips moving again and guessed the question. 'How long? It is now near to the end of March. I think you should be up and walking by the end of next month. Fit enough to travel back to England by the end of the month after that. You will be in time to see most of your cricket matches. Eh!'

Though it couldn't be evening yet, the room seemed to be getting dark. A pleasant lethargy spread over his limbs. But, there was something that he had to say. Something that couldn't wait. Anna leant over him, to try and catch the faint words.

'Peters. Krauts'll turn this city upside-down about this raid. Bound to find out about English. If tries to go . . . if tries to get out alone. Get him. Tell father you must watch him and stop in house here. Till . . . till I'm well again. You understand?'

She nodded, feeling a tear gather at the corner of her eyes. 'Don't worry, Pan Standish. It will all be as you want.'

'Bloody better. Otherwise. Know what I'd do? Don't you Anna? Christ, turn the light on. Bloody dark!'

His head sank back on the pillow, and he fell into a deep sleep.

Zbigniev poured himself another drink.

The doctor closed his bag with a click that sounded unnaturally loud in the quiet room.

Anna pulled up one of the straight-backed chairs and sat down beside the bed.

Leslie Peters, plucked from the unfriendly hands of the Gestapo, drew hard on the cigarette, and coughed as the cheap tobacco rasped at his throat.

Across the city, Herr Stürmbannführer Neumann sat alone in his office and wondered what the day's raid would mean to his plans. He flicked a speck of dried blood from the top of his desk.

CHAPTER EIGHT

The weeks dragged by. The weather remained beautiful, and trees bloomed. In the small apartment, nerves began to fray. Peters proved an ill-tempered guest, nagging and moaning at every opportunity. He made one pass at Anna, and was smartly rebuffed by having a pot of near-boiling water poured over his legs.

Standish gradually clawed his way back to health, faster than the doctor had expected, but nowhere near as fast as he himself had wanted. The collar-bone was soon well, and the gloomy prognostications about internal bleeding proved to be false. But, when the bullet struck the ribs, it had thrown off a number of tiny chips of splintered bone which caused patches of infection in the chest.

In the end it proved necessary to bring an anaesthetic into the flat and operate on him for the removal of these chips of bone. The flat stank of ether for three days afterwards, which gave Peters yet another cause for complaint.

By April 12th, he was taking his first steps, though the doctor had advised against movement. By the end of April he was ready to move. But, there had been a major operation against the Underground in the Warsaw area and travel passes were impossible to get. So, the date for their move was set at Wednesday, May 8th.

During the waiting, Anna and Standish had been unable to get much time together. Zbigniev had followed his instructions and made sure that Peters was watched at all times. Though he protested to Standish about it, he got little satisfaction.

'What you have to understand, Leslie, is that we don't know all that much about you. All I was told by London was that you were a pretty important man who knew more than was healthy about the Polish Resistance. We have reason to believe that the Gestapo are now aware of your importance – that's why the searches have been so thorough. If you were caught out, or if they intercepted a phone message from you to a friend, it could mean the deaths of many brave men and women. So, Zbigniev had his phone cut off to remove any temptation, and I've given orders that you stay here until you leave with me. Sorry, old boy.'

Peters curled his lip and turned away. 'Well, I suppose you know what you're doing, old boy. But, frankly, it seems a lot of fuss about nothing. Even if they caught me, they'd never get a peep out of me.'

'You bloody fool, Peters! Suppose you were tied out naked on a table, with some big Nazi beating your balls to a bloody pulp. Systematically destroying your manhood. Turning you into a mewing eunuch.'

Peters waved a languid hand. 'All right. No need to go into the details. I still think I'd hold out longer than some of these niggers and froggies seem able to.'

'Sometimes, Peters, "old boy", you make me want to bloody puke!'

Twice, the two Englishmen had been forced to crouch in the fake water tank in the Cybultna loft, while heavy boots stamped about them. Several of the escapees had been recaptured by the Germans, and they were hanged at the corners of main streets as encouragement to the others not to transgress the party line.

The news that filtered through on the old man's forbidden short-wave radio from England was not good. Despite inept intervention from the Allies, the Nazis had easily walked over Denmark, and Norway had fallen in barely longer time.

There were reported rumblings in Parliament about the failure of English troops to put up more of a show, and there was even talk of demanding the resignation of Prime Minister Chamberlain. Apart from the sad failure of his proud boast of

'Peace in our time', he had claimed in the House on April 4th that 'Hitler had missed the bus'. Only one day later, General Ironside, the Chief of the Imperial General Staff said: 'Our army has, at last, turned the corner ... We are ready for anything that they may start.'

But, it hadn't, and they weren't. This galling news of black failure piled on disaster, prompted even greater impatience from Standish. It was obvious to anyone with half a brain that Hitler wasn't just going to squat on the other side of the Belgian, Dutch and French borders, smiling pleasantly and passing the time of day. Standish felt that a move could only be a matter of days away, and it was an unbelievable relief the day that Anna brought the news that they could finally leave on the 8th. The Germans had relaxed their watch, and papers were again available.

The night before they were due to go was a melancholy occasion. Peters had pleaded a mild headache and had gone to bed early to rest up ready for the next few days' tension and exertion. Zbigniev had brought out a fine bottle of old brandy and the three of them sat round the small table, getting a little drunk.

The old man climbed to his feet and proposed a toast. 'My beloved Pan Standish. My dearest daughter, Anna. As the clouds darken over the world, I fear that I will not live to see the coming of light again. No, I know what I'm talking about John. I can feel death in my bones. I would ask one thing of you. Although she occasionally strays from the path of virtue, Anna is not a bad girl. You silly goose, do you think you can hide from your own father when you are in love? And when a man has given you a toss in the blankets. It could have been a worse fellow than this lanky Englishman here.'

Anna and Standish looked at each other, but neither of them spoke. It was a time when words would not be appropriate.

Zbigniev went on: ' Look after her, John, when I have gone to join my beloved Maria. And my boys.' He pushed back his chair and went over to his bedroom. 'You know John. This world under Hitler. I don't think that I really want to carry on living – or, existing – in it for any longer. Tomorrow, you have to go. Tonight, I expect that I shall sleep well. So soundly that I would not hear anyone moving about in any of the rooms. Dobranoc, my children.'

Moved by the dignity of the old man, Standish went quickly to him and held him in a close embrace, marvelling at the frailty of his body. As they stood close, Zbigniev whispered in his ear. 'Be gentle with her tonight, my son. The parting will be long and she is still only a child.'

Standish kissed him formally on the cheek, feeling the stubble rough in the furrows of the old man's face, where it had become difficult to shave.

'Goodnight, my father, You have no need to worry about Anna as long as there is still breath in my body. Thank you for everything.'

Zbigniev stooped and kissed his daughter on the top of her head, while she clasped his hand in hers and wept a little. Then, he was gone.

That night, Anna came to his room and they made love until the first light broke over the summer city.

When Standish got up the next morning, Zbigniev had already gone out to work at his garage. Peters was late getting up, and was in a foul mood, moaning that his teeth were hurting him. He hadn't bothered to pack the previous night, so Anna and Standish had to help him.

Both men took the minimum of luggage, to support their story that they were welders, being called out of their Warsaw homes to do an urgent job in Breslau – at the aeroplane factory there. A quick look round the apartment that had been their home for too many weeks, then they left. Anna was to drive them out of Warsaw to Lodz, where she had relatives, and where they would catch the train.

At Standish's suggestion, Anna was to stay in Lodz for ten days, only returning to Warsaw on May 19th. After he had tidied up the apartment and cleared up a few things at his garage, Zbigniev was to join her. Friends would keep an eye on their home and make sure there were no Gestapo spies snooping around.

She dropped them off outside the city and she and Standish made a brief and embarrassed farewell under the cynically amused eyes of Peters. Then she drove off.

There were no challenges in Lodz, and they caught their train with no trouble. Both men spoke fluent Polish, so there was never a need to risk the charade of one of them having to pretend to be a deaf-mute, as there had been with Jean.

They were in Breslau by noon. There they met an obstacle to their plans. They had intended to catch a train, under a different set of papers, which would have taken them clear across Germany, through Leipzig to Bremen in the north. From there it would have been a short hop to the Dutch border, and Standish reckoned that it would not prove hard to slip undetected across. Somewhere near the River Ems.

The face behind the ticket window was thin, with narrow eyes, half-hidden behind gold-framed glasses. 'I don't know why the line is closed, but it is. If I knew, I doubt if I'd tell you. Though,' the voice grew confidential. 'I did hear a whisper about a lot of troop movements over in the west. A despatcher friend of mine said that the lines have been choked for weeks with tanks and men and guns flooding towards the border. If you ask me, I think it's going to be the big push through Holland into England. Then we'll show all those greasy Jews. That Jew Chamberlain. Their Jewish King and Queen. Those Jewish politicians. Did you hear that the umbrella man had retired? True. Anyway, I can't sell you tickets any further than Leipzig.'

Standish made some lightning calculations in his head, trying to visualize the map of Europe. 'What about Stuttgart?'

The man checked his list, hanging from a bent hook at his elbow. 'Yes, Stuttgart is all right. Through Prague and Nürnberg. Third class? You get in at eight tomorrow night.'

While they sat drinking lemon tea at the station restaurant, Peters argued furiously with Standish. 'Look here, old boy. I don't fancy getting trapped somewhere in the south of Germany. Why don't we go back to Warsaw. Safe flat there. I mean, where the hell can we get to from Stuttgart? Answer me that, old boy.'

A previous occupant of the table had spilled milk on the scratched top. Using his fingers, Standish drew a sketch map of where they were going.

'There's Stuttgart. Here, to the west, but only a bus ride away, is Baden Baden. I was there taking the waters in thirty-six, and I got to know the area thereabouts pretty well. It's only a spit from the frontier with France. We can get a train and be in Paris in one day. Look up Jean Marreq, and spend a day resting and making contact with London. We should be strolling down Pall Mall by May 11th. Cheer up. Don't look so damned miserable, Leslie, old boy. How about another cup of this dreadful liquid? No? Suit yourself.'

It didn't quite work out as Standish had predicted. It was fine in theory. But, while they were on the starting-stopping train snailing across Europe, Hitler's crack troops were preparing for their great attack westwards.

They were held up for a miserable day in Prague; it was half-day closing; it was raining. And, they had a run-in with a gang of Czech youths who thought they were German spies.

The train didn't leave until late afternoon on Friday, May 10th, by which time German troops were pouring over the frontiers of Holland and Belgium. As they neared the French border, Standish noted vast camps of men and machines, cleverly camouflaged from air observers. Security checks multiplied and they were several times to bless the combination of the Polish Underground's skill at thieving and Standish's own supremacy as a forger. Their fake papers passed every single test.

'Looks like the big push is coming here any day now.'

Peters looked bored. 'Teach the Froggies a thing or two. No doubt they'll start shitting their trousers the moment Adolf shouts "Boo" at them. Just like they did in the last lot. The lads I feel a bit sorry for are the boys in the B.E.F., stuck there without a hope in hell of holding up those ace German regiments. They'll be over-run in a matter of days.'

There were many things about Leslie Peters that it was difficult to like. In fact, the longer Standish was forced to spend in his company, the more he realized that it was difficult to find anything to actually like about the man. Still, he had been doing undercover work among the Poles for the best part of a year. And he'd been in the hands of the Gestapo for weeks. Anyone's nerves were likely to be all shot to Hell after that sort of experience.

Finally, the waiting was over, and they got through to Stuttgart. From there it meant waiting over-night for the bus to the frontier and Baden Baden.

The weather had changed again as they walked the hills together near the famous spa. The sun shone, and a hawk soared effortlessly on a thermal high over their heads, a dot against the blue. Though they had seen sentries thick as flies on a cow's arse down below; here on the high meadows, they were alone. It was absurdly easy to slip over the frontier that evening.

At four o'clock the next day they walked out of the Gare de L'Est on to the Rue d'Alsace. Standish hailed a cab and they were driven at breakneck speed to Marreq's flat.

Waving a finger at Peters to caution him to silence, Standish rapped loudly on the hunchback's door, shouting out: 'Open up! Come on you little sod! It's the police! Open up or we'll shoot the door down!'

There was a shuffling inside, then the rattling of a chain. The door opened an inch and an eye peered suspiciously out at them.

'John, you bastard! I didn't know you were going to be in Paris. I thought you'd go out through the north. Wait a minute while I open the door.'

There was more clanging of chains and slamming of bolts, then the door was flung open. Standish grinned, 'I thought you might be out. In fact, you took so long, I thought you were never coming.'

'I was beginning to think so too, Monsieur,' said the naked girl, lying sweating on the sofa.

CHAPTER NINE

Later that night, after the girl had cooked them a superb stew, then left, they exchanged news. Marreq bore no grudge for the way Standish had overcome his pigheadedness and got him out of Warsaw. He sniggered into his wine over Standish's description of his brief phone conversation with Neumann.

'I bet he thought the bloody ceiling had fallen in on his head. In that case, I find it not the least surprising that the whole of Warsaw was in an uproar after you plucked Monsieur Peters from the Gestapo. More wine, Monsieur; we must drink yet again to your escape and perdition to the invading Hun.'

Peters rose unsteadily to his feet and drank. The flush on his cheeks showed the effects of a surfeit of wine, yet he carried on, mixing in frequent glasses of brandy. After the toast, he walked around the apartment, flicking idly at Marreq's bits and pieces. He opened the door of one room and whooped with amusement at what he found.

'I don't believe it. You're a bloody painter! Aren't you?' He lurched back into the dining-room. Stood over the small figure of the hunchback. Waving his glass of brandy extravagantly, so that some of the amber liquid sprayed over on the carpet, he poked his finger into Marreq's chest.

'I bet I know who you model yourself on, my tiny Froggie. I bet I know.'

Standish saw with an awful clarity where the conversation was leading and stood up. 'Peters! For God's sake, man! Sit down and shut up.'

But, he was not to be stopped by words. His speech slurred, he carried on. 'Bet I know.' He laid a finger alongside his nose, trying to indicate the depth of his cunning. 'You're like that other little Froggie. Lautrec. Old Too-Loose. Eh? What do you say?'

There was a moment's stillness. Marreq's face had gone rigid, his eyes flickering about the room, as though seeking some familiar object to focus his thoughts on. Standish clenched his fist, ready to either strike down Peters or Jean.

'Jean! I ask you, as a favour, to remember that this man is important to defeating the Germans. Many lives have already been lost to get him this far. If I thought that his life was in danger, I would do anything; anything, Jean, to keep him safe. All right?'

Even in the extreme of his anger, Marreq could hear and understand the stress in his friend's voice. Peters vaguely realized that something was wrong.

'I say, old boy. Didn't mean anything by that. Just a little joke, don't you know. After all, he was a painter like you, and he was ... sort of unusual. Eh!'

Marreq smiled with his lips, though his eyes were as cold and distant as the steppes of Siberia. 'Monsieur Peters. I beg that you do not concern yourself with what you have said. It is true that Henri Marie Raymond de Toulouse-Lautrec was a painter. In fact, I would be pleased to think that I were one half the artist he was. Or, one quarter the lover.'

'What! Didn't think you were doing so bad there when we came in.'

Quickly, Standish changed the subject to what had been going on in Europe in the last crowded week. As he did so, he flashed a wink at Marreq, and was grateful to get a grin back.

The Germans had made their usual blitzkrieg attack on the neutral Low Countries. Marreq agreed with Standish that it could only be a matter of hours before France was subjected to the same treatment.

'Frankly, Jean, I have my doubts whether our boys in the B.E.F. have much of a chance against Jerry in that sort of war. Too many of our generals are living in the days of trenches and salients – barbed wire and "Over the top" at dawn. Hitler's Panzers will cut them apart while they're still trying to dig a foxhole.'

Peters lifted his head with an effort from a pool of spilled wine on the table. 'That ticket-clerk fellow back in Poland. Didn't he say that Chamberlain had gone? Bloody good job. Man's a fool. What we need is Halifax. Fine fellow. Knows what's what.'

Marreq got up and walked over to sit at the long sofa. 'From what I hear through my friends, it will not be Halifax. Two days ago a National Government was formed. Under Churchill. Here, it was reported at length in this morning's paper.'

Marreq's news got no response from Peters, unless a hog-like snore could be called a reaction. Sighing, Standish left him lying and went to sit next to Marreq.

'Jean. About Peters.'

A wave of the hand stopped him. 'John. You and I know each other well. What you say about that man is true. So, I will help you get him back to England. But, I would not be averse to altering the shape of his face if he ever returned to Paris. When he insulted me, my first reaction was to kill him where he stood. Strike him down in his arrogance. But, I bought an early copy of the works of Lobkowitz at a stall on the Left Bank. Through the red mist of hatred that blinded me, I thought of something he said, and it calmed me. He said: "If a man stares at the noon-day sun, and calls others to come and witness the vision he sees. Then, the man who joins him is a ten-fold fool." '

Standish laughed. 'I suppose you're right. Must say I'm not enamoured of the chap. Still, we'll be away tomorrow morning and be home by nightfall. What's the matter, Jean? Have I messed up some plan or other?'

'Tomorrow evening, I have a few people coming round here. Men and women who feel the inevitability of war and are already preparing ways to resist. Since you are here, I thought you might stay an extra day and perhaps talk with them. You know much more than I how one can fight against an invader.'

The figure at the table gave a loud snore and slid inelegantly from the chair, cracking his head on the leg of the sofa as he did. The snoring stopped briefly, then resumed with added vigour.

'I thought the pig might have killed himself. Leave him there. It's his natural habitat.'

'About these people. They shouldn't know who I am. Just tell them I'm an Intelligence officer from England. Yes, I'll do it. One more day won't make that much difference. Since you've been reading my mentor, maybe you can remember his words on the subject of guerrilla fighting. No? He said: "A man with a gun may think himself unbeatable, yet he can be defeated by a handful of fleas." I'll tell them that.'

The evening went well, marred only by the shadowy presence of Peters, lurking on the fringes of the group, insinuating an occasional comment, and drinking heavily from a brandy bottle.

Standish was impressed by these potential resistance fighters. They were all aware of the risks they would be likely to run. Most of them had some form of weapon, and they were all prepared to fight and to die for their country.

He and Jean demonstrated ways to kill a man silently and efficiently. They showed them how a simple fire-bomb could be made out of a bottle of petrol, a couple of spoonfuls of sulphuric acid and a bit of calcium chloride taped to the side.

Peters thrust his way to the front, his breath stinking of drink and said that he would tell them what is was all about. He stunned Standish by giving a brilliantly lucid and informative talk on how to set up a net of cells, linked in each case by only one man, so that no one was able to betray more than a few others.

When he had finished, itemising communications, arming, sabotage, use of children and women, carriers, coding, drop-points, printing, murder and subversion – the whole pattern of Underground fighting – there was silence. Then, the senior man there, an old bar-keeper named Pierre Godard stood up.

'Tonight we have seen many things that will help us if the Boches take our country, and we have heard much sound advice. But, of all, the greatest help has been Monsieur Peters. We would not wish to have any finer men to aid us in the struggle. On behalf of everyone here, we thank you.'

Peters said nothing, remaining slumped in the armchair, clutching his bottle of brandy as though it were the true elixir of life.

After they had all gone, Marreq and Standish sat together in the living-room. Peters had fallen asleep on the sofa, the lines of worry on his face smoothed out in rest.

'I was wrong in some ways about him. I thought that he was just a shit. Now I know that he may be a shit, but he bloody knows his job. I should have guessed that Tristram wouldn't have given anyone a job just because of the 'old boy' network. He made it sound so easy. He told them what they wanted to hear.'

He was suddenly aware that Peters was awake. His face was flushed, and marked with red where he had been resting it on a crumpled cushion. His eyes were swollen, but his voice was completely cold and clear.

'Yes, I told them, didn't I, old boy? About what a jolly lot of fun and games it was going to be. You know, there was actually a time when I believed all that shit. I really thought it would be like something out of the "Boys' Own Paper". High jinks against the stupid squarehead. Lovely women trying to worm secrets out of you over a slipper full of best quality champagne. Dinner suits and a Smith and Wesson. Pat on the back from a grateful King. Oh, sweet Mary! I really believed all that.'

To Standish's embarrassment, Peters began to weep; great lumps of tears coursing their way down his cheeks. Quite unnoticed. Marreq got up and went out into the tiny kitchen, leaving the door open.

Ignoring the tears as though they didn't exist, Peters carried on talking, his voice at a normal conversational pitch. 'You know what? I should have lifted up that romantic picture and showed them the black loneliness and corruption that lies on the other side. The nights without sleep. The bowel-wrenching terror of making a simple pick-up, when you imagine that every tree hides a Gestapo agent. Feet on a stair, a casual glance on a crowded bus; no friends. No medals. No rest. Always having to look over your shoulder. Trusting nobody. Afraid to even screw some little street slut, in case you fall asleep and cry out in English. My God!! If only they knew what I know. If they had seen what I've seen. They'd go home and start making swastika flags instead of bombs. You know, Standish, don't you? Why the hell did you feed them the old line?'

'Because, they'll find out for themselves. It's better to try and to fail, than not to bloody try at all.'

Banging his hand on his knee to give stress to his words, Peters shouted his reply. 'Wrong! Fucking wrong! I lived in Warsaw for months, hardly seeing a soul. Frightened to go out in case I got picked up. I'll tell you what Resistance work is like. I had a carrier in Warsaw – young married woman with a son. Her husband had been killed fighting on the eastern front. Someone must have wanted bigger food rations, and they betrayed her. The Germans came round to her apartment and started to interrogate her. That slimey bastard, Neumann, it was. She denied everything, so they took her up town and gave her the treatment. Pulled out her toenails, broke her fingers, drilled all her teeth down to the gums. Oh, you know! She wouldn't talk. So they brought her little boy in. Neumann sat there at his big mahogany desk and told her in his quiet voice what he'd do to the boy, in front of her, if she didn't talk.'

He stopped for a moment. Marreq had come back in, and stood in the doorway, a silent spectator.

Standish spoke quietly, when the silence seemed as though

it would go on. 'What happened?'

'She asked if she could be alone with the child for five minutes, to try and explain what was happening. To try and make him understand. Neumann thought he'd won, and agreed. The Germans waited outside. All they heard was the woman talking in a low voice. Then the breaking of glass. By the time they got back in it was too late. She'd picked up the boy, holding him somehow in those broken hands, and jumped. She was eight floors up. They were both killed instantly.'

Finally, he became aware that he was crying, and tugged out a white handkerchief and wiped his face. 'That's what it's all about. They'll win in the end, because they are more ruthless than we are. More skilled at fear. Better at inflicting pain. Every man has a weakness. A spot that can be probed until he loses all reason. It doesn't have to be pain. I met a writer bloke out in India. Blair. Eric Blair. He used to talk about it till he drove me potty. There are some things a man can't take. Things he has to have. Everyone has their own little weakness. Everyone."

And he collapsed, sobbing, hiding his face in the cushion. Marreq sat by him, stroking his shoulders as one would a young child. 'All that is over, my friend. For you, I think there will be no more fighting in this war.'

Standish's voice cracked across the room. 'What about you, Peters? Did you have a breaking point? Did you have a price to pay?'

The question hung in the air, slowing time, waiting for an answer. Finally, Peters sat up, pushing Marreq's arm away. A shadow had fallen over his face, covering up the emotion.

'Me, old boy? Not me. Can't say if they had got round to me. But they didn't. You saw that for yourself. No, I'll never know what my particular raw nerve is. That is, if old Blair was right. I say, sorry about this. Tension, I suppose. Must get an early night tomorrow. Are we off then?'

'No. There's a couple of things I want to help Jean out with tomorrow. We'll get to the coast on the fifteenth. Hop a boat then. Incidentally, I don't want you wandering all over Paris. Your papers aren't correct. Jean is getting something done about that. In the meantime, it'd be stupid to get picked up by the flics just as we're nearly home.'

'Oh, bloody hell! I'm getting tired of being cooped up in shitty little rooms. If I want to go out, then I'll bloody well go.'

'I'm sorry, Leslie. Really, after what you've been through, it must be tough. Still, I think that Jean can arrange for someone to come and keep you company.'

'Keep me prisoner, you mean.'

'Have it your own way. Now, I'm tired as well, and I'm not going to go through this bloody argument all over again. You stay here. Now go to bed.'

With a little help from Marreq, Peters staggered off to his room, still muttering rebelliously. After he was quiet, Standish had a last peaceful drink with Marreq.

'John.'

'Yes.'

'Peters. A strange mixture. A fool and a cunning and able man. There are times when I hate him and times, like just now, when I feel a deep sorrow for him. I think that he is a man who has been through a dark place.'

'And come out again?'

'That, my friend, I do not know.'

Marreq left the apartment early the next day, leaving John to wait with Peters until the 'friend' arrived. Pierre Godard's son had been contacted and had agreed to come and sit in. When there was a knock at the door at nine-thirty, Standish confidently expected it to be the boy.

Instead, it was a pert young girl, in her late teens, wearing a pretty summery dress of flowered gingham. Her hair was a natural ash-blonde, and she wore it in the fashionable short curls, tied at the back with a length of black, silk ribbon.

'Yes, what can I do you for?'

She smiled uncertainly. 'You are Monsieur Constant? My name is Patrice Godard. My father is Pierre Godard.'

He opened the door wider and invited her in. 'Well, at least come in and tell me what you want. I was expecting your brother.'

Peters had come in to the room, and stood, in his pyjamas, grinning at the girl. 'Yes, Monsieur. Sadly, he fell off his bicycle this morning and has sprained his ankle. So, if it's all right, I have come instead. My father wasn't all that pleased, but I told him that I would be as safe with Monsieur Peters as anywhere in Paris.' She saw the look of doubt on Standish's face. 'Please let me stay. My father has told me what I am to do.'

He turned to Peters. 'Well, Leslie? Do you give me your word not to try and leave against the wishes of Mademoiselle Godard?'

Had he been sporting a moustache, Standish could have sworn that Peters would have twirled it. His hand actually went to his upper lip, then came down again as though he had only just remembered he was clean-shaven. His voice, when he answered, had that growl to it, so beloved of British actors when trying to indicate their approval of a pretty girl.

'John, old boy. It would be a positive sin to leave such an attractive flower to bloom all alone here. Yes, by all means. You have my word that I won't leave here as long as Patrice indicates she would rather I stayed.'

It was well into the afternoon when Standish returned to St. Germain-des-Prés. The elderly concierge was waiting in the street, looking anxious. When she saw him, her face lightened.

'Aah, Monsieur Constant. I'm glad you are back. I hoped that Monsieur Marreq might have been here.'

'What's wrong?'

'Oh, nothing, Monsieur. I'm sure there's nothing. It's just that I heard a bit of noise as I was cleaning my own room this morning. It seemed to come from Monsieur Marreq's apartment. Now, I'm not one to pry, but when I went up the stairs, I couldn't hear anything at all.'

Standish edged past her, towards the stairs. 'Probably they knocked something over up there. My friend Monsieur Peters is sometimes a little clumsy. When I get there I'll ask him and I'm sure he'll have an explanation. Now, if you'll just . . .'

But, the old woman hobbled after him, catching him by the sleeve. 'He's not there.'

He spun round so sharply that he almost knocked her over. The look in his eyes was so angry, that the concierge recoiled from him, raising her arm as though to avoid a blow.

'What do you mean; he's not there? He must be.'

'No Monsieur. Ooh, have I done wrong? I didn't know. What shall I do if Monsieur Marreq is also angry with me?'

Seizing her by the arm, Standish shook her as one would a rag doll, so that her hair came unpinned and her teeth rattled in her skull. 'When did he go out? And did a girl go with him?'

The old woman was now trembling so much that she could hardly force the words through her chattering lips. 'He ran past me at about ten o'clock this morning. And, he was on his own. Oh, another thing. There were scratches on his face. Or cuts. Perhaps he shaved in a hurry.'

Standish paused outside the door of Marreq's apartment, gathering his breath. The teachings of Tao Chu-Wen came to his aid, and his hand was steady when he turned the handle of the door and walked in. Quietly, he pushed the door shut behind him.

The apartment seemed empty. All the doors were open. The small table with the elegant bronze flying horse had been knocked to the floor. The cover was ripped off the sofa and trailed on the floor. A brandy bottle lay on its side against the heavy radio, with a broken glass by it. There was still a thick, sticky deposit left in the bowl of the glass, where two flies were contentedly gorging themselves.

A girl's shoe was visible under the sofa, and a torn piece of cloth that might once have been a blouse. His feet making no sound on the heavy pile of the carpet, he walked across the living-room. In the doorway of one of the bedrooms was another scrap of cloth. Standish bent down and picked it up. It was a pair of knickers. Stained with blood. He crumpled them up and threw them on the floor.

The room was empty. The bed was a shambles, with blankets and sheets ripped and on the floor. The bottom sheet was half on the bed and half on the floor. A brown patch in the centre of the mattress was also blood. Standish's shoe kicked at something under the bed, and he bent down again. With a cluster of blonde hairs still trapped in the knot, it was a length of black, silk hair-ribbon.

His face a bleak mask of taut anger, Standish walked back into the living-room. The passing of his shadow disturbed the feeding flies, and they flew tipsily around the lightshade.

Apart from the buzzing of the flies, there was another noise in the apartment. He put his head on one side, as he strained his ears to catch it. Very faint. Seeming to come from the bathroom.

The sound of crying. Someone sobbing to themselves. Softly and monotonously.

A young girl.

Standish closed his eyes and took three deep breaths. Then, he opened his eyes.

And walked quickly into the bathroom.

A week later, and Peters still hadn't reappeared. Not a word had come of his existence. Nobody had seen him. No one knew where he was. Marreq had put out his own net, reinforced by the blazing efforts of Pierre Godard and his own circle of friends.

The news that Hitler had made his planned move against France on Friday, May 17th, passed almost unnoticed. A message came from Bowditch wanting to know what was going on, and ordering Standish back to London. With or without

Peters.

He stayed where he was, helping the searchers.

Marreq had tried to persuade him to go back, but he had ignored his advice. 'Jean! I brought him to Paris. The very least I can do is try and find him and get him out. If Godard gets to him first, then he's a dead man. And, it'll all have been for bugger-all.'

The hunchback looked at him, and said quietly: 'I have told you, John, what I will do. It is something that cannot be ignored or glossed over in the name of what we have always called "friendship". That is not a word I use lightly, and I know that it is a word that you too value. But, I tell you this, my friend. A girl, a mere child, full of all the freshness and innocence of youth. Enjoying the first summer of being a young woman. Here, in my apartment, on my bed. She is beaten-up and raped. Not once, but several times. Things are done to her that I would not wish to hear about if they were done to the most scabrous and wicked whore in Les Halles.'

During the quiet, bitter speech, Standish sat still and silent.

'Then, her body torn and trembling, she drags herself into my bathroom and hacks away at her wrists with one of my old razors. All right! I know all about resilience. She is alive, and her cuts and bruises are going. I could become trite and say that it is her inner scars that will never quite vanish. It is trite, but it is true. Now, that is why I try so hard to find Peters. When I do, or one of my friends do – and they will, John, there is nowhere big enough to hide a rat in Paris that will not be searched. Then, I will talk to him alone for a long hour or two. Then, I will let Pierre talk to him. If you can get to him first, then you may take him.'

Standish stood up. 'Everything you have said is true, Jean. We both know it, but it is better that you remind me of it. You know what I must try to do, and why I must try to do it. After ... well, we shall see. If I do this, what will...?'

'What will I do? Nothing, John. I will regret that your duty lies where it does, but I will understand it. You have my word that it will never, ever come between us.'

At the door he paused, and his face was grave. 'I do not think I would be able to make that promise for Pierre Godard.'

The Panzer divisions still ground their inexorable progress westwards. Holland had fallen on the evening of the day that Peters had vanished. By Friday, May 24th, the situation on the Continent of Europe was bleak. Belgium could not be expected to hold out for more than another five days, and France was being torn apart by Axis armour. The British were flocking back towards the Channel. More or less the whole of the survivors of the Expeditionary Force, with a large percentage of the French Army, were in full retreat, facing the moment when their backs would be up against the sea.

It was obvious to any strategist that no naval operation on earth could have the slightest chance of saving other than a handful of senior officers and a few key personnel.

To the south, Mussolini had done all he could to make the trains run on time and was now casting envious eyes at the success of his Fascist brother dictator. An addition to the Axis family was expected at any day.

And all of that mattered less to John Standish than one ravished girl, and one vanished spy.

And, on the Friday, Leslie Peters got in touch. Just as Standish was leaving Marreq's apartment, a thin urchin sidled up to him with a scrap of paper. He was about to take it, when it was snatched away.

'He said you'd give me some money for this.'

Feeling in his pocket, Standish gave the brat a handful of loose change. In exchange, he got the note. As the child scampered off, Standish shouted after him. 'Hey. How did you know who to give this to?'

Before answering, he picked something out of his nose and popped it in his mouth. 'He was English like you. He said to give it to the tall Englishman who came out of that house.

Anything else you want to know? Right.'

The note was brief and to the point. Scrawled in thick grocer's pencil, it simply said: 'Five ack emma where Foch's road runs into the woods. Monday. P.'

Standish woke at three on Monday morning, dressing quickly and quietly. He had written a short letter to Marreq the night before, and he propped it on the dining-room table against a bottle of best brandy he had bought on the Saturday.

The letter was to the point, simply stating that he had been sent a note from Peters, and that he was going to meet him at an agreed rendezvous. It ended: 'If things get too warm for you in Paris, come and see me. I will always welcome you. Thanks for everything. Lobkowitz said: "I would rather welcome a bitter enemy, than bid farewell to a true friend." Goodbye. John S.'

He was lucky enough to get a cab, and it dropped him off at the Place de l'Étoile. It was nearly four. One of those misty, warm mornings that shows the city at its romantic best. Taking his time, he strolled up towards the Avenue Foch, turning towards the distant blur of the Bois de Boulogne.

The streets were completely deserted, apart from the far-off wailing of a police siren. He walked alone, involved in his own thoughts.

Where the road ran among the trees, the moonlight gave a fairy, ethereal quality to the wood. Most of the trees were heavy with blossom, and he breathed deep. It was half-past four.

Without looking round, he spoke quietly. 'You can come out now, Peters. You've had the chance to see I didn't bring anyone.'

'Good job, really, old boy. Might have been unfortunate all round.' There was the unmistakable sound of the hammer of an automatic pistol being eased off, and the click of a safety catch engaging.

Standish finally turned round. Peters looked tired, but

otherwise in good shape. He was shaved and wore a suit that looked second-hand but good quality. The scratch marks on his face were barely visible.

'Hello, old boy. Look, I'm sorry about the Frog wench, but she...'

He stopped as Standish deliberately turned his back and walked a few paces away. Over his shoulder, Standish said: 'I don't want to know at all. Patrice told me about it, after they'd set her jaw. I'll get you back to Bowditch and then that's it. If I ever see you again, then I promise you that I will make every effort to kill you.' The voice had such steel in it, that Peters shivered. Though the morning was warm.

'That is not an idle threat. Life is too short for such futile exercises. So, believe me, Peters. I will kill you if I see you. Now, I think we'd better be going. Marreq and his friends have been combing Paris for you. When Jean wakes up and gets my note in about two hours time, he'll blow the whistle on us both. Let's go.'

'Where?'

'One of the Channel ports.'

'Christ, haven't you been listening to the radio over the last few days?'

He wheeled round. 'I've had other things on my mind over the last few days. What?'

'The German Sixth Army, and Five and Seven Panzer Divisions have surrounded the B.E.F. near the coast. Bits of the French and Belgian Army are still just about functioning. You really didn't know? Our only chance is the coast east of Calais. Near Dunkirk!'

CHAPTER TEN

In the end, it was a 'borrowed' car that got them through the closing corridor that led to the sea. By the time they reached Armentières, the radiator was boiling and they were nearly out of petrol. It was late afternoon on Monday 27th May.

Twice they'd been stopped – the first time by a firmly-disciplined British unit that was controlling the crowds wanting to flood through to the sea. A brisk young captain established their bona-fides in a matter of a couple of minutes, waving them through. They were obviously British, and there were a number of nationals who had left it to the last minute on that road. As they were moving on, Peters asked the officer what would have happened if he hadn't believed them.

'Pull back the tarpaulin for these gentlemen, sergeant,' he'd replied. Behind the canvas sheet, were the untidy sprawled remnants of about a dozen people. 'Jerry paratroopers, sir. Not very convincing, though.'

'Jolly good, old boy,' said Peters weakly as they drove off.

The French unit that stopped them were a different matter. Led by a dishevelled N.C.O., smelling strongly of wine, they were ready to shoot them both out of hand. It was only when Standish relapsed into some of the worst gutter argot he could remember from his Montmartre evenings with Jean, that they took their fingers from the triggers of their 1886 model Lebel rifles. And stood, gaping open-mouthed at the flow of filth vomiting from the mouth of this self-confessed English milord.

So, they went on.

Armentières was in ruins. It had been heavily shelled by the Germans, and most of the main buildings had been wrecked. These included the town lunatic asylum, and the streets were lined by the escaped mad men and women. On one corner, they saw a young girl, with heavy eyes, green snot dribbling down her mouth, sitting with her dress round her waist, while she rubbed herself with filthy fingers. All the time she gave a low laugh, rising every now and again to a shrill scream.

A corporal from the Forty-second Division saw them looking at the girl and grinned. 'Bit unnerving, innit, seeing all these nutters about the place. Still, time like this I reckon anyone still here must be a bit barmy. Her? She's the one we give a nickname to.'

Standish grimaced. 'Don't tell me, corporal. *Mad*moiselle from Armentières. Right?'

'Got it in one, sir. Anything at all I can do for you gentlemen?'

'Petrol?'

'No chance. Anyway. You don't really need it. Hitch up on any of these lorries heading north. There's only one place to go and that's out.'

'What's happening on the beach?'

'Very well organized, sir. Navy's done us proud. They're shipping the lads off in ships you'd never believe. I seen one of the old paddle ferries myself. Here, I'll stop this lorry and you can both swing aboard. Good luck.'

The lorry took them to within ten miles of Dunkirk, then it was walk. As they strode along together, Standish and Peters watched amazed at the scenes on all sides. Though the Army had been shockingly defeated, there was still order amongst the chaos.

Teams of men were calmly and systematically wrecking the mountains of equipment that lay in huge dumps. Wireless sets were lined up in rows while a soldier with a shovel went along, smashing the front of each. Trucks were demolished – the engines crushed with pick-axes and sledge-hammers, while tyres were slashed. Finally, they were set afire. The smoke from this colossally expensive funeral pyre soared over the area.

It was full dark when they got near to the sea. Standish was in a lot of pain from his old chest wound, and found little sympathy from Peters. They tagged along with what was left of a company of the King's Own Scottish Borderers, waiting patiently in line to cross the last canal between them and the beaches.

Though there had been sporadic attacks by German fighter-bombers, the R.A.F. had been doing their stuff up above the clouds and the position wasn't as bad as it might have been. There was a muffled cheer as the news was muttered back down the line that the bridge still stood.

Then it was a fumbling march through the night, lit only by an occasional star-shell, through the ruined village of Malo-les-Bains, and over the useless railway line. Broken glass crunched underfoot, and the way was lined with the hulks of some of the first trucks that had got there.

Suddenly, Peters fell on his face with a curse, twisting his ankle. 'What the fucking hell is this?'

A rich Scottish voice answered from just in front: 'Cheer up laddie. It's sand. You're on the beach.'

With Standish's chest and Peters' twisted ankle, they were, for once, in agreement that it might not be a bad idea to stay put and wait for the morning before looking for an embarkation officer.

They found a comfortable spot in the lee of an overturned armoured car, and both slipped into an uneasy sleep. His training kept Standish on the knife-edge of awareness, despite his extreme exhaustion, and he was instantly awake when he felt Peters move.

'Where the hell are you going?'

The voice was aggrieved: 'Good God, Standish, old boy. Just because you don't happen to like me. I mean! I was just going for a quick Jimmy Riddle.'

But, there had been the glint of moonlight on steel.

For the rest of the night, Standish slept with his foot just touching Peters' leg. It was enough contact for the slightest movement to waken him.

He woke just before dawn, to find Peters still in a bad mood. 'What do you think? I'm going to run off and leave you all alone.'

Standish smiled a thin, grey smile. 'No, "old boy", but I can just see a possibility that you might be worrying about me spilling the beans about your rape of that child.'

'What! In that case, why did I bother to get in touch with you again? Eh, answer me that?'

'Easy. You stayed somewhere in Paris – one day I'll find out where – and waited until the last possible moment to contact me. You want to get back to England, and I'm the best man around to get you there But, now we're on the beaches, you might get the idea that I'm dispensable. Incidentally, relax about what happened in Paris. I'll not tell Tristram, if you don't. That'll be our secret.'

Dawn showed the dreadful panoply of death and destruction on the beaches of Dunkirk. The dunes were sprinkled with dead and dying, the smell as the summer sun rose higher resembling nothing more than a huge slaughterhouse. Packed like colonies of ants, soldiers clustered together in their units, afraid to drift away from their mates in case their turn came for a place on a ship and they weren't there.

Beyond the beach, the row of houses that had once graced a bustling promenade now stood like a row of burned teeth, with a gap here and there where high explosive had removed one. Stretching out into the sea was the massive stone shape of the Mole. Ships already darted alongside, collected their quota of men and made for the comparative safety of the open sea.

The first Stukas of the day appeared from the south and flew low over the beaches, dropping bombs, and then strafing the fleeing troops. Amazingly, these raids, with virtually no retaliation, caused few casualties.

'Bloody poor shots, these Jerry pilots,' observed Peters from the safe cover of the armoured car.

'Be a different story if this was a rocky beach. The bombs and shells are just plopping into the soft sand like eggs into flour, and they aren't fragmenting at all. Thank God!'

The first wave of attackers vanished, and Standish got to his feet. 'Come on, Peters. I think it's time we were on our way.'

The Mole was a mass of struggling humanity. Tommies and poilus mixed in together – some with rifles and full equipment, and some with only the stinking remnants of uniform. Within ten yards Standish saw a diminutive Welsh lance-corporal wearing nothing more than a flowered bath towel tugged about his dignity, with a ferocious-looking German cavalry sabre hanging from a leather belt. Next to him, as immaculate as though he were waiting to crash on to the parade ground at Caterham, was the erect figure of a regimental sergeant-major, holding nothing more combatative than a polished swagger stick.

As the two civilians pushed their way through the troops, they attracted a lot of odd glances. Finally, half-way along they were stopped by two corporals with fixed bayonets. Beyond them, the chaos became order. A haggard-faced officer stood by a small desk, covered in piles of paper, weighed down with stones from the beach.

Peering at the man, Standish thought the face seemed familiar, and shouted past the soldiers: 'I say. My name's John Standish. Didn't we meet at Everilda Woodfleet's twenty-first in January?'

The eyes swivelled, and the brain struggled to meet this extraordinary greeting. From the charnel-house of Dunkirk beaches to a party in Northumberland was a massive leap, but the officer was equal to it. He smiled and half-rose as though to come over to them, then sat back and shouted to the corporal: 'I think you may let them through.'

They joined him, ducking as a wave of dive-bombers swooped low overhead on a strafing run. Over to the left, a small yacht exploded in a burst of yellow fire. Nobody took much notice as the boat joined the dozens of other wrecked craft scattered about the sea.

He held out his hand. 'Howell. Mark Howell. Good to see you again Standish. How are things? Bit hairy round here at the moment. Sorry we can't offer you a sherry or anything.'

Standish grinned and introduced Peters. Then took Howell by the shoulder and moved a little away. 'I'm on an S.O.E. job. Just got back from Warsaw. I'd be grateful if you could fit us in somewhere as soon as possible.'

Howell looked thoughtful, then bellowed to another officer further up the causeway: 'Two quickies here, Jamie. What's going?'

Another explosion sprayed a wave of grey salt water over them. Howell cursed as some of his papers vanished into the sea.

Another officer, wearing a German helmet, stumbled up to them. 'Blast! You've just missed one of the Southern Railway Channel steamers. "The Maid of Kent" just sailed. Next one out is a private yacht from London. She's crowded out with over a hundred men already. Come on, I'll ask the skipper to take on a couple of supernumeraries.'

There was just time for a quick hand-clasp for Mark Howell, then they were away again. Dodging between lines and groups of soldiers. Just before they reached the embarkation point, they passed a platoon of men carrying rifles from which they had carefully removed the bolts and thrown them into the sea.

Their tin-helmeted guide grinned cheerfully. 'Fucking idiots! Blokes do odd things in this sort of situation. Saw one fellow with a pack full of false teeth. Couldn't even remember where he got them from. Here we are. "Pinnacle Dawn". I'll just clear it with the skipper.'

While they waited, the two men stared silently at the scenes on the beach. Tens of thousands had already been evacuated, yet there were still at least a hundred thousand left. Smoke from the region behind the dunes, where the destruction of mountains of equipment was to go on to the last possible moment, hung – a huge question mark over the area. It was like a gigantic nursery, where a wilful child had scattered and broken all his toys and soldiers, then trampled them and burned, in an attempt to make them disappear.

Peters looked at Sandish, and the flippant remark died on his lips. His eyes looking beyond the desolation, the leader of 'The Killers' was thinking of all the friends he was leaving behind. Men and women of his organization struggling to keep a little light burning in all the countries occupied by the Nazis.

Jean in France, Zbigniev and Anna in Poland, Johann in Holland. Of Gunther in Bavaria, forced to pretend glee at the German victories. Sven in Norway and Gina in Naples. And Andy. God knows where Andy was? Last Standish had heard he was in Tokyo, but he might equally well be in London or Calcutta. Or even in his own home in Los Angeles.

All united in their common hatred of oppression. Yet, at that moment, all very alone.

Sixty feet long, with a maximum speed of twelve knots, the 'Pinnacle Dawn' had sailed from Ramsgate with dozens of other small boats. She had only the most minimal protection from the over-worked Navy, and carried only out-of-date charts which didn't show the minefields – and no armaments at all.

She was commanded by a retired naval officer named Patrick Trippett, D.S.C., R.N.R., a keen amateur sailor, who had heard the news on his radio about the plight of the retreating British Army. He had instantly freed his boat from her moorings at Twickenham and sailed to Chiswick. From there it had been a short haul to Southend, then into the crowded waters of the Channel.

The troops were packed below decks like sardines in a can. There were men in the bunks, under the bunks, in the microscopic galley, in cupboards. There was a man sitting cramped on the toilet seat and three huge Scottish gunners in the bath. Complete with three rifles and two bren guns! Trippett was a bit vague about who would do the navigation, and Standish offered to lend a hand. An offer that was gratefully accepted.

Peters found a niche for himself in the lee of the wheel-house. They cast off the bow and stern lines, and chugged slowly from the Mole. 'Pinnacle Dawn' was so crowded that she handled like a pregnant cow, wallowing in the lightest cross-swell.

Trippett cursed and sweated, wrestling with the wheel whenever a larger vessel – a destroyer or a minesweeper – cut past them, sending her bow-wave crashing over the low deck. Peters soon got very wet and began to moan, so Standish suggested he went below. Pale-faced and clutching at his stomach, he accepted the suggestion gratefully.

Grinning back over his shoulder, Trippett said: 'I doubt he'll be better off. Bit like Dante's Inferno down there. Still, good luck to him. Both in Intelligence, are you? My son was going to try for that, then other things came up and he finished up in the Navy. I'm not sorry about it. Runs in the family, you know.'

He was interrupted by the return of Peters, whose face had now assumed a light green shade. At first, he couldn't speak, his mouth opening and shutting like a ventriloquist's dummy. When he finally managed to speak, his voice was high and strained. 'God! Christ! Down there. How in the name of God are they putting up with it?' By now they were well out into the Channel, dodging wrecks and dive-bombers, and Trippett was kept busy sending his boat lurching from side to side. Despite the blue sky and warm sun, the sea was distinctly choppy.

'The whole thing's a mass of vomit. They're all covered in it. Chunks of regurgitated bully beef and stale biscuit. The floor's inches thick in swilling puke. Oh, my God! I'd rather get washed overboard than go down there again. The only sane ones are three Jocks sitting solemnly in the bath passing round a bottle of whisky they've liberated from somewhere, singing "Amazing Grace" in unison.'

Nearing the English side, they ran into a mine-field, with the horned spheres appearing to bob up right under their bows. Standish spent one of the least pleasant half-hours of his entire life lying on his stomach in the bows, ready to fend off the mines with a cracked boathook.

A Junkers 87 gave them a few nasty moments when they were only a couple of miles from the coast, coming in low and trying to strafe them. Trippett was desperately worried by the attention, but Standish reassured him by going to the stern and watching the plane as it made each run. The Junkers needed a twelve degree elevation to bring its guns to bear, and Standish simply waited till he saw the nose start to lift and then gave the order to turn. After three runs, the pilot was obviously getting frustrated and came in even lower for his fourth run. 'Port this time, skipper!' shouted Standish, waiting the moment.

Just as he shouted, a sten gun went off a foot from his head, making his ears ring. The 'Pinnacle Dawn' came round sharply to port, and he was thrown over to the starboard quarter. A hand grabbed at him – or, pushed at him? – then he was on his feet again.

'Got the bastard! Saw bits flying off him!' The voice, the shooting and the hand, had all been Peters'. Sure enough, the Junkers, trailing smoke from the engine, was side-slipping as it tried to gain height. The smoke darkened, as oil ignited, then the flames spread to the fuselage.

There was an explosion like a fire-ball, then the plane tipped into the sea, its starboard wing catching the top of a wave, sending it cartwheeling down in a cloud of white spray. Peters was jumping and laughing, his sickness forgotten in the elation of the moment.

The rest of the trip was comparatively uneventful, though

they were delayed outside Folkestone harbour while the authorities tried to sort out the mess of small boats flocking backwards and forwards. It was only when Standish made a couple of flags out of a broken broom-handle and two handkerchiefs, signalling that they had one hundred and forty-three men on board, that they were waved in.

Standish and Peters stood out of the way on the bridge with Trippett, while the troops filed off. Or, in some cases, were carried off. Most were in a fearful state, after days of retreat, hard fighting, exposure on the sand dunes of Dunkirk and a crossing of unimaginable awfulness. But, their spirits were still high as they clambered unsteadily off the little boat. Under the command of the senior N.C.O. present, one of the Scots, they drew themselves up in ranks on the narrow jetty.

"Attention! As you were. Come on lads. One more time. Attention! That's better.' The lines of weary and defeated men were suddenly transformed into soldiers again. Eyes brightened and shoulders went back. 'I would ask you for three cheers for this very gallant gentleman and his grand wee boat. Platoon, three cheers. Hip, hip, Hurrah.'

As the cheers rang heartily out, Standish was not at all surprised to see Trippett surreptitiously wiping his eyes. 'Seem to have a bit of grit in my eye,' he said. Unconvincingly. He waved to the troops as they marched off.

'Grand bunch of lads. Things look pretty black at the moment. But, you can't beat them, you know. I wouldn't give a bent pin for Hitler's chances when some of that lot get back over the Channel at him.'

He reached over and switched off the engine. The calm was quite deafening, with only a handful of gulls circling above the harbour. He wrinkled his nose. 'Fair old cleaning job I've let myself in for. Still, have to get her ship-shape. Catch the tide tomorrow morning and pick up another load.'

On the way across, Trippett had talked a lot about his son, in the Navy. Now, as they left him absently rubbing a piece of cotton waste over a brass fitting that had somehow got greasy,

Standish had one last thought.

From the jetty he shouted down to the elderly man. Still erect after a day of tension and gut-ripping effort. 'I say, sir. Your son will be jolly envious when he hears about all this gallivanting you've been doing.'

The white head didn't lift in acknowledgement. Then, finally, Trippett did look up. 'Thank you for the thought, Standish. Fact is, my son was killed on the 'Hardy' in the raid on Ofot Fiord. Narvik. Seven weeks ago. In the middle of a snowstorm, they said.'

The London train was already packed, but one of the soldiers – a Cockney private – recognized them and waved them over.

'Come on, sir. Last leg of the trip now. Reckon we can just about squeeze a couple more in here.'

Standish stood aside to let Peters on first, then followed him into the crowded compartment. A group of lady volunteers had been handing out free cigarettes to the returning troops and the air smelled heavy with Woodbine smoke. They squeezed into a couple of seats and sat and waited. More Tommies came heaving their way in, all cheerful now that the nightmare in France was over.

Each new arrival was greeted in exactly the same way by the private, still hanging out of the window. Finally, it became too much for Standish.

'Private! If you say "Anymore for the Skylark" just one more time, I shall take your head and ram it right up your arse. Right?'

'Right,' said the soldier, not in the least put out by the threat. But, at least he stopped saying it.

The train disgorged them at Victoria, and Standish and Peters quickly got away from the milling mob of soldiers, into the relative quiet of a pub in Buckingham Palace Road.

Wiping his mouth after the first pint had slipped down easily, Peters gave an appreciative belch. 'Very good, old boy. First real drop of beer in over a year. Worth waiting for. And, the second should be just as bloody good.' He leaned over confidentially. 'What's the score now, old boy? I mean, when do we get to see Tristram?'

Standish sipped more slowly at his first pint, savouring the clean, bitter taste. He had been wondering himself just what the answer was to that question. Since he'd ignored Bowditch's requests to travel back from Paris, he had no idea what his reception would be.

Still, he consoled himself. He was a free agent, and his allegiance was at best a loose one. He'd brought back the bacon, intact, and that was the main thing.

He drained the glass and stood up. 'Now. We'll get a taxi and go and see Bowditch right now.'

They caught a taxi without any trouble on the corner of Eccleston Street. Standish gave the driver the address – at the back of Barnard's Inn, Holborn – of Bowditch's offices, and sank back on the faded seat. Peters coughed, and then straighened his shoulders, bracing himself to speak.

'Before we get there, John, old boy.'

Standish groaned. 'What the hell is it now? You're not going to ask me about Patrice Godard again are you?'

He nodded. 'Well, you know what would happen if . . .'

Prodding him in the chest with his bony fore-finger, Standish interrupted him. 'One last time. Letting you get away with that makes me feel dirty, as well as letting down some good friends. But, there are priorities and you come high just at the moment. And, I meant what I said before. After today, when I leave you to Bowditch's care, I never want to lay eyes on your contemptible person again.'

He suddenly grabbed him by the throat with one hand, making his eyes pop out of his head. Squeezing, tighter, till the breath gargled in Peters' throat. 'I will fucking kill you if I see you. Like the vermin you are. I don't care what you did for the S.O.E. in Warsaw. I know that you would have killed me on Dunkirk beach if you hadn't been so shitless scared. And, I know that you tried to stage an accident on the boat. Right.

Now, shut up.'

The rest of the journey was completed in silence. Peters sat massaging his neck, where the marks of Standish's iron fingers stood out like purple splashes.

When they reached Holborn, Peters got straight out of the taxi and walked through the gates towards the office. Standish paid off the driver with the money he'd borrowed from Trippett on the boat over.

The driver, muffled up despite temperatures in the high seventies, poked a finger at the departing Peters. 'You and him had a bit of an argument?'

Standish looked after him, seeing the hand still rubbing at the throat. 'Yes. Frankly, I think he finds me a pain in the neck.'

Bowditch had greeted Peters warmly, seeming a little reserved at Standish's appearance. After drinks and a brief social chat, he sent Peters off with one of his aides to be taken to their Hertfordshire headquarters for an extensive debriefing. Before leaving, Peters made a major production of shaking Standish's hand. 'Can't ever thank you enough, old boy, for all you and your little chum did for me. Immensely grateful, you know. I'll never forget you. No doubt we'll meet again. Cheerio.'

'Don't know where, don't know when,' muttered Standish, wiping his hand on the side of his trousers.

Bowditch saw the gesture. 'Gather you and he didn't exactly hit it off, John.'

'You could say that.'

'Still, you brought him back and that's the only thing that matters.'

He put down his drink. 'Is it Tristram! Is it really? Well, with the greatest respect, let me tell you that you are wrong. It just happened to be the thing that mattered most at the time. But, it was *not* the only thing.'

Bowditch poured him another sherry, then sat down in the

other deep armchair. 'I'd like to hear about it. Not all; that can wait. But the main things. I was bloody worried when you didn't acknowledge from Paris. I suppose that was one of the "other things" you mentioned.'

So, Standish told him. Not everything. Not the rape. But the raid, his wound, Marreq's part in it. The state of the Resistance movement. Bowditch interrupted him once to tell him that he would be getting a top priority weekly report from a new Polish agent who had been dropped in only a few days ago. His first message was due on Thursday at noon.

The only other interruption was when an officer came in and gave Bowditch the news that Belgium had just surrendered.

King Leopold had announced that he intended to stay with his defeated people. Unlike Queen Wilhelmina of Holland.

'Only France to go now. How long do you reckon?'

Before replying, Standish had to count on his fingers to make sure he knew what day it was. Having decided it was the 28th, he answered Bowditch. 'I give them until about the fifteenth. Once Paris goes, that'll be it. Il Duce can't wait to get in at the spoils. He's like a bloody jackal, licking his lips while the lion does all his dirty work.'

'Is that one of Lobkowitz's sayings?'

'No. A Standish original. When you get the news from Poland, give me a ring. Let me know how Zbigniev and Anna are getting on.'

'All right, John. I'll do that. Fancy a bite to eat tonight?'

'No thanks. I'm going to get stupefyingly pissed, then I might arrange to be carried round to the good Mrs. Protheroe's salubrious establishment and indulge myself in the desires of the flesh.' He put the glass on the oak table and walked to the door. 'Christ! I'm bloody tired after this one, Tristram. It was a mess in too many ways. Sloppy. Still, it's over, and not too many of our people got hurt. That's about the only good thing I can find.'

And, he went out, leaving the door open, and walked into the sun.

Anna and her father had enjoyed a relatively peaceful time in Lodz, marred only by a German raid on the old Jewish quarter of the city. They kept in touch with their friends in Warsaw, and were relieved to learn that the Gestapo activity had died away.

They returned, as agreed, on May 19th, opening their apartment again. The rooms still smelled of dust and Anna threw open all the windows. Although there was depressing news from the Western Front, there was still hope within Poland.

Resistance groups grew busier, blowing up a troop carrier in the south of the city, and assassinating a senior Gestapo officer on the 21st.

In retaliation for the last killing, S.S. troops swooped on Pilsudski Square and arrested one hundred Poles as hostages. They were to be shot in batches of ten every morning if the killer of the Gestapo man didn't give himself up.

All hundred died. The Underground also had their own retaliation. During those ten days, nearly fifty Germans were shot, garotted, knifed, blown up, or, simply vanished. It was at this time that there first appeared the slogan: 'Kazdy Pocisk Jeden Niemiec.' 'A German With Every Bullet!'

They were not happy days for Stürmbannführer Neumann. His life became a bleak round of reports of killings. Until, near the end of May, he received a telephone call.

'Speaking ... why have you not called before? ... what ... very well.'

His hand, still wearing those sinister black leather gloves, reached out for a pad of paper, pulling it to him. Then he picked up a stubby fountain pen and began to write.

'Those are all the names? ... They will do ... Are you coming back? ... No, I would prefer it if you did not ... It will be paid by the usual means ... Of course.'

Impatiently, Neumann tried to cut the conversation short. The light from his reading lamp glinted back from the thick smoked lenses of his wire-rimmed spectacles.

'Very well. Now I must follow up all these names starting with the old one. Once you are settled, contact me again. I think we can again do business. Goodbye.'

He put the phone down and looked at the list of names neatly written on his pad. And a smile clawed its way on to his lips, and hung there like a rictus of unspeakable pleasure. Neumann tapped his fingers soundlessly together, then pressed the button of his intercom.

That evening, Zbigniev Cybultna was working late in his garage, when he heard the click of boot-heels. He straightened up, rubbing the small of his back. Facing him were four Nazi soldiers, wearing the death's-head symbol of the S.S. At their head was a short man, in the black leather coat and soft hat that had become recognized as the uniform of the Gestapo.

'Your name is Zbigniev Cybultna?'

He wiped some of the oil off his fingers, stalling for time. Trying to think what had happened. Whatever it was, it looked bad. Anything to do with the Gestapo was always bad.

To delay in answering was a mistake. The Gestapo officer made a sign to one of the troopers, who stepped smartly forward and crashed the barrel of his Schmeisser sub-machine gun into the old man's groin.

He moaned and fell to the floor, retching for air.

'Obviously he is. Take him to the car and then search this dump.'

His eyes watering with pain, Zbigniev was vaguely aware that he was being dragged, feet trailing, across the garage and out into the street, where he was flung into the back of a car. His lips framed the one word: 'Anna', when a boot heel jabbed hard down on the back of his neck, smashing his face to the floor. He lost consciousness.

At about the same time, Anna was hurrying back to her apartment from a friend's house. She carried a small quantity of gelignite in her bag, ready for a raid that her group were planning the next night.

As she swung round the corner of a narrow alley, close to home, an arm seized her by the throat, and a hand clasped over her mouth, silencing her scream.

Not a word was spoken.

CHAPTER ELEVEN

For the whole of Wednesday, Leslie Peters went through an elaborate and careful debriefing, supervised by Bowditch himself. Where, when, who, how were the questions most often asked, though Bowditch was careful to slip in an occasional 'Why?' as well. It was obvious that Peters had done an excellent job, right from the start. He'd made the right contacts, and built up several groups to pose an effective threat to the Nazis.

He enjoyed his lunch. The country headquarters was a large house, in a secluded position in East Hertfordshire, overlooking the lovely village of Stanstead Abbotts. The food was good by any standards. For war-time, it was magnificent. A clear soup, followed by grilled trout, followed by some excellent beef. Dessert was strawberries and real cream.

'Wonderful, Tristram,' he said, cleaning a stray trickle of cream from his chin.

Bowditch smiled at Peters' obvious delight. 'Fine. Fine. No more than you deserve. Now, we'll have a drop or two of a rather good port they keep for me here, then we'll retire again to the Library. We're just coming to the part that interests me most. The week or so before Jerry got to you. The time you were with the Gestapo, and then all that happened after John sprang you.'

The two men leaned back in their chairs, while a servant brought in a crystal decanter of port.

The water in the bowl was stale and brackish, but Cybultna lapped it up eagerly. He lapped it up, because his hands had been handcuffed behind him from the moment he had been arrested, apart from the brief occasions when they allowed him to go to the toilet. He lapped it eagerly, because it was the first liquid he'd been allowed in nearly three days.

He wondered if it was day or night. Where Anna was. Who had betrayed him. When they were coming to hit him again. He knew his limitations and he was aware that he would not be able to hold out for very much longer.

Some of the water went down the wrong way and he coughed. In the light from the naked bulb, he could see that his spit was flecked with blood. It had been warm when he had been brought in. Now, he felt cold. They had stripped his clothes from him at the first interrogation. Or, had it been the second? It was no longer easy to distinguish one from another. Sometimes there was brutality, sometimes, they seemed kinder. They had told him that they were just preparing him for their boss.

Tomorrow, he would meet Neumann. He shivered uncontrollably. His naked body was a mass of bruises and burns. His thighs were discoloured and purple from beatings, and his genitals an oozing mess of flesh. One eye was closed, and he thought that they had punctured one of his ear-drums. As he moved to a sitting position in the corner of the cell, he caught the raw ends of his fingers on the rough concrete and tried to scream.

But, the lack of liquid had made his tongue swell and the only sound was a muffled moan. And all that there was to look forward to was tomorrow. In some way, the worst of it was the journey along the corridors to the interrogation rooms. He was rarely conscious for the return journey to his cell.

Naked and manacled, they dragged him past offices full of young girls, who laughed and jeered at him. Once, a girl had spat at him, and hit him in the face with an ebony ruler. And she had called him 'Traitor. Fool. Killer.'

In Polish.

If she had been German it would not have been so bad. He dropped his head to his arms and slipped into a sleep, crowded with nightmares.

Mrs. Protheroe had run her house in Half Moon Street for over twenty years, catering for at least half of every Government and a fistful of the crowned heads of Europe. Discretion was her middle name, and she would provide anything a man could ever dream of. At a price.

In the days when Standish was less well-known in county circles, and when his career as an international forger was still in the first flush of its youth, a friend had come and asked him to help out a lady who had run into a little problem over some share dealings. The help involved some delicate work on some share certificates and bonds, and the lady had paid handsomely.

She had also taken young Standish under her wing and helped him on a number of occasions. The lady, of course, was Mrs. Protheroe. Now in her sixties, she was an impressive figure. Nearly twenty stone, with a head of white hair that owed nothing to her hairdresser and everything to Nature. When she was really dressed up, for a Gala opening or a Premiere, she looked stunning.

It always amused her to sit in a private box and count her customers thronging the stalls. Standish sometimes accompanied her, for the sheer pleasure of her talk. She trusted Standish implicitly and told him the most scurrilous gossip about the sexual manners of eminent men of power. Gossip that she would never have revealed to a High Court Judge. Yes, she had those as clients as well.

She had been delighted to see Standish when he appeared on her doorstep that Tuesday evening. He was stinking drunk. A bunch of orchids clutched tightly in his hand. These he presented to her with a grand flourish that endangered his perilous balance. But, even drunk, John Standish remained the gentleman.

'My dear Mrs. Protheroe, how delightful to see you again. I would be eternally obliged to you for the hire of a bed for the night.' He saw her mouth open ready. 'No, Mrs. Protheroe. Just a bed for this night. I have been removing a damnably unpleasant taste from my mouth and I would now like merely to sleep.'

She still stood looking at him. Shaking her head. 'John Standish. You look like a man who's had a nasty time, but I never knew that stop you having a lay. Are you getting past it?'

'Past it, Mrs. Protheroe? I have not even reached it. Indeed, you can always read me like a book you evil lady. Very well. At eleven tomorrow you may waken me with a chilled white wine and a plate of devilled kidneys, in a best silver chafing-dish, mind. Then, one of your most lovely new acquisitions.'

'Only one?'

Standish looked shocked. 'Of course, only one. Unless – do you still have those sisters, the Indian girls? No? Pity. In that case I'll settle for your newest and best. Providing she has the skill with the ...'

Mrs. Protheroe nodded. 'Of course. I know just the thing. Then you must join me for afternoon tea. I'll get some Darjeeling and a few scones and you can tell me all you've been up to.'

'Right. After that I shall again avail myself of one of your beds and one of your young ladies. As usual, I make the suggestion that you might care to join us.'

Mrs. Protheroe laughed, her chins quivering like sacks of pink jelly. 'Go on. One day I'll take you up on that and then you'd have a shock.'

Halfway up the grand staircase, he paused. 'You know, Mrs. Protheroe. Lobkowitz said: "The body of a fresh maiden is like a bounteous garden, where an honest man may long sport at his pleasure!"'

'Well?'

'I just say that there's no substitute for experience. Don't forget to come and tuck me in.'

During the next twenty-four hours, forty-seven thousand Allied soldiers would be plucked off the beaches of Dunkirk.

Many of the armada of small ships were hit. Among those posted as missing was the 'Pinnacle Dawn'.

In Paris, Jean Marreq was busy carrying out a contract. A private job for someone who had heard of his talents from a Chinese merchant. Now that he operated as a freelance, Marreq could afford to choose his contracts with care. Nobody who was honest need apply to him. No husbands who wanted to be rid of jealous wives. Only the big-time. Only the criminals.

This time it was an influential pimp who was worried about the inroads being made into his business by a Corsican rival. So, enough money had changed hands, and the rival was now only seconds away from the end of his life.

Patiently, Marreq waited in the shadows, his hunched shoulder hidden by the blackness. The long, thin garotte cord hung loosely from his hands.

Back at his apartment there waited an unfinished painting of 'Death At The Feast Of The Sibyl', and another small treat. Although he found he didn't need it anymore, the occasional use of heroin stimulated other pleasures. A gift from an old friend now lay in a sealskin pouch in a drawer in his kitchen.

He giggled quietly to himself at the thought of what a good evening it was turning out. Then he stopped. His sensitive ears had caught the sound of steps walking rapidly towards him. He gripped the handles of the cord, and prepared himself to spring.

Leslie Peters went for a walk in the quiet grounds of the S.O.E. house on that Wednesday evening. The weather was still superb. It was after midnight, but the temperature was still well over seventy. The smell of laburnum came to his nostrils.

The day hadn't gone that badly, though the afternoon had worked less well than the morning. He had asked whether Bowditch had made any arrangements to have him replaced by parachuting someone else into Poland, but he felt that Tristram had dodged the question. Still, he shrugged it off, there was only one more day there, then he would be free to lose himself in the crowds of some big city and do what he wanted. There was three months leave waiting for him.

It was unusual for them to insist on a physical immediately after a mission, unless there was something obviously wrong with an operative. Apart from the wrenched ankle at Dunkirk, he was in fine shape. Bowditch had told him to take the morning off, stroll around the grounds. Then report for a medical at one and meet him for lunch at two.

Still that nagging doubt, nibbling away in one of the rooms at the back of his skull where he didn't normally go. He walked on, wondering. Maybe ... if he went off now. Could always say it had become too much and he had to get away.

Down through these trees, there used to be a gap in the wire. There.

'Halt. Who goes there?'

'Friend.'

'Come forward, friend, and be identified.'

Peters walked slowly towards the sentry, cursing under his breath.

'My name is Peters. I'm staying with Bowditch.'

A hooded torch gleamed briefly in his eyes, then went out. 'Very well, Mr. Peters. I'm afraid that nobody is allowed beyond this inner perimeter without a pass. I suggest you return at once to your quarters.'

Argument with a man armed with a loaded rifle didn't seem all that profitable. So scuffing his feet through the leaf mould under the trees, Peters went back to the room provided for him by S.O.E. and got to bed.

Where he passed a reasonably peaceful night.

In his cell, Zbigniev Cybultna did not sleep. He had been interviewed by Neumann. The Gestapo officer had not once laid a finger on him. He had begun by apologising for the ill-treatment that he had already received.

'You see, Herr Cybultna, they are such enthusiasts for their work. Why, it was all I could do to persuade them to let me talk to you at all.'

The pleasantries were brief. Neumann walked about the room, rubbing his chin with his gloves, his eyes impenetrable behind the tinted glasses. Then he stood alongside Zbigniev, and gently stroked the injuries he had received. Talking in a low voice.

'Dreadful. Such an old man too. Oh, those fingers! They look as though someone has broken them. And that eye's bad. I fear you might lose the sight of it. The trouble, Zbigniev – you don't mind if I call you Zbigniev? The trouble is that we must all get old. Even those fine, muscular, mindless young thugs that I am forced to employ. And the body becomes so frail. And so easily hurt.'

Cybultna sat silent, trying to blank his mind off from that insidiously evil voice. But it was impossible. It went on and on.

'This will be the only chance I get to speak to you like this. Tomorrow it will be all shouting and hitting. Gouging and tearing. Look what they've done to you there. It must be agony even to pass water.' His hand brushed against the old man's groin.

At last, the Pole spoke. 'May I say something, Herr Stürmbannführer?'

Neumann squatted down by the side of the chair where Cybultna was manacled, naked. 'But of course. Nothing would give me greater pleasure than to hear you say as much as you wanted. That is why you are here. To talk to us and tell us what you know. Now?'

Despite his beatings, the old man's voice was still quite strong. 'When I was beaten, it hurt me a great deal. When your men humiliated me, I also suffered. But, the touch of your hand is a greater obscenity. You are a stench to my nostrils and I would be happy if you could end this quickly so that I may enjoy the simple pain of your comrades.'

Even though his lips were torn, and the inside of his

mouth lacerated, Cybultna managed to spit in the German's face.

But, it was another wasted effort. Neumann took a clean handkerchief from a drawer of his desk and wiped off the thread of saliva. Then, he carefully wiped the old man's mouth as well.

'You see, Zbigniev. It is futile to resist. Did you think I would fall into a fearful rage and stamp and shout? Because you spit on me. No.'

He walked away and sat down, watching the Pole's head droop to his chest.

'Did you even hope that I might become so maddened with anger that I would put you beyond our reach by killing you? That would be too easy. There are things that we must talk about. Since it cannot be now, then it must be tomorrow. But, then we will have someone else with us.'

Neumann let the statement hang in the room, nibbling at Cybultna's mind. Until the old man had to ask.

'Who else?'

The Gestapo officer smiled and clapped his hands softly together. 'Good. Good. You are still interested in things. As a reward, I will tell you. Tomorrow morning, you will again come to this room, but you will not be hurt. The hot rods, the hooks, the truncheons, the needle – none of them will be for you. All you will have to do is to sit quietly and watch someone else suffer. A pleasant change I expect. And, another treat. If you want to stop this other person suffering, all you have to do is speak, No, less than that. Merely nod your head. I will be watching you closely, and when I see that signal, I will immediately order my men to stop. Then you can talk, and then this, this other person will go free. And, you? You will be shot.'

He strolled over to the window and surveyed the summer afternoon. Then, he looked back. 'You see, Zbigniev, I do not insult your intelligence by telling you I will spare you if you confess. You are a partisan and a murderer of Germans. You choose the way you fight your war, and I salute you for it. But, you must now pay the price for living with yourself on the terms that you have willed.'

Cybultna tried to speak, but his tongue was dry. He licked his lips and tried again. 'Who is this other person?'

Neumann put his head back and laughed. A healthy, clean laugh of a man genuinely amused. 'Zbigniev! You have a lovely daughter, Anna. Do you know where she is?'

The look on the old man's face showed the answer too clearly. 'Of course, you didn't. Tomorrow, you may see her. First you may have a chance to talk to me. Don't answer now. Go back to your cell and think it over. You may have some clothes to wear, and I will arrange for those cuffs to be taken off for one night. Go now, and think it over.'

As the guard raised the Pole to his feet, Neumann came to him and stood very close. Without warning, he placed one hand on each shoulder, and kissed the old man on the head, as a son would kiss a father. In a low voice, so that no-one else could hear, he whispered: 'Think tonight. It would hurt me to destroy your only daughter.'

In his Half Moon Street room, Standish lay with his head pillowed on the firm breasts of Mrs. Protheroe's best whore. The sheets on the bed were black silk, and a large mirror fixed to the ceiling enabled him to watch himself. Clinically, he looked at his own body, noting how he had lost muscle tone during the tedious confinement and recuperation in the Warsaw apartment.

After he'd seen Bowditch tomorrow, he'd catch the overnight sleeper up north and spend a couple of weeks on his estate. Plenty of walking, a little swimming. Regular exercises and lots of good cooking and fresh air. Then, he'd be himself again.

He was distracted by gentle fingers moving slowly down over his stomach. At least *that* was still in good working order. 'Good God, girl! Don't you ever rest?'

She giggled and rolled him over on to his front, sitting astride his back, massaging his shoulders with her hands. 'Perhaps you would prefer a quieter time?'

With a buck of the body, Standish rolled back over. Hanging on by pressing her thighs round his body, she grinned impudently down at him. Reaching behind her, she held on to his swelling maleness, stroking it. His left hand played with breasts, enjoying the feel of the hard nipples as they rolled between finger and thumb. With his right hand, he massaged the silky inside of her thighs, rubbing higher and higher. When his hand reached the damp centre, she moaned and threw her head back.

He probed inside her loving body, using first one and then two fingers. It was too much for her, and she suddenly raised her body, and lowered herself on to him, guiding him deep inside her. He hissed in through his teeth at the tightness that gripped him, then he began to move, thrusting deeper and harder.

She responded to his passion, raising and lowering herself over his hips. 'Careful it doesn't slip out. I wouldn't fancy having you grind down at the wrong angle. Ruin me for life.'

Without any warning she hopped agilely off and scampered to the bedside table. 'Hey, it's rude to leave without even saying "Goodbye". I shall speak to Mrs. Protheroe about your manners, you young ... what's that?'

She had picked something out of the drawer, and was now readjusting herself on him again. Leaning back, her fingers had probed deep between his legs. But, thinking better of it, she sat forward, showing him what she had in her hand.

'This'll be really something. I learned it from an Oriental gentleman Mrs. P. had in a week or so ago. I bet you like it.'

'It' was a short length of string, with knots tied at intervals along it.

Standish raised his eyebrows. 'What on earth do you propose to do with that? Where? No! I don't care if ... does it?

All right. Have you ever heard of a man called Lobkowitz? Well, he was a wise man, who said: "The man who constantly rejects the new, must spend all his life with the old." So, go ahead.'

In the next room, Mrs. Protheroe took her eyes away from the small hole for a few moments, to freshen up her glass of port and lemon. Then, smiling, she returned to watching.

CHAPTER TWELVE

The clothes that Zbigniev Cybultna had been given to wear were the filthy rags that had been stripped from some other unfortunate. But, at least they kept him warm. And, Neumann had kept his word. For the first night since he had been taken by the Gestapo, the Pole had his hands free of the manacles that had left a bloody scar round each wrist.

But, they were not likely to risk losing their best hope of breaking the entire circle of partisans in the Warsaw area, by letting him do away with himself. His feet remained bare, and the trousers had no belt. Obviously, the shirt had no tie and the pockets of the jacket had been thoroughly searched to make sure there was nothing in them that would give the prisoner the least chance of killing himself.

As skilful killers themselves, the Gestapo were equally cunning at ensuring that their victims had no opportunity to kill themselves. The cell had no windows. No bars. Nothing at all protruded from the walls to enable a determined man to hang himself. No bed was provided, just a thin mattress that lay directly on the floor. The one blanket that he had been given was too short and too narrow to cover the whole body, and only provided a minimum of warmth from the middle of the chest to the centre of the calves.

The light, covered with a bolted grille in the exact centre of the ceiling, had a thick glass shade and remained on all day and all night. The steel door was perfectly smooth on the inside, and had a round Judas-hole near the top, through which all special category prisoners were watched at frequent intervals through the night.

The cell, concrete-walled and floored, measured precisely two metres by two metres, and was three metres high.

Cybultna lay on his back, as prescribed by the authorities. Any attempt to turn on one's side or face was punished promptly by a rifle butt in the groin, or a slash across the face with the heavy bunch of keys carried by all the guards.

Though the Gestapo were thorough, they sometimes made mistakes. They hadn't realized how frugal and careful the average Pole was. Prepared for any contingency, the previous owner of the jacket had hidden a small safety pin behind one of the lapels.

Zbigniev had found it, and now held it in his right hand, clumsily and painfully gripping it between his broken fingers.

Ready.

Thursday, May 30th, 1940, dawned just as warm and sunny as the rest of the month had been. The sky was clear and blue. A nightingale dived and sang in the dawn air.

Leslie Peters was woken first by a servant bringing him a cup of tea and the morning papers. After he'd drunk it, the warmth overcame him and he slipped back into sleep. The second time he was woken was at ten by Bowditch. Outside his window he could hear the steady whir of a lawn-mower. He breathed in the fine, green smell of newly cut grass and grinned at Bowditch.

'Lovely day to be alive, old boy. Oh, to be in England and all that sort of thing. Eh? Didn't expect to see you before our luncheon date. Two o'clock isn't it?'

Bowditch nodded. 'Right. Since we didn't see you at breakfast, I assumed you'd decided to have a bit of a lie-in. Thought you might fancy a game of squash, to get you set up ready for the medical. I've got something on at twelve, so we should be able to have a brisk match, then have a shower after. Then, it'll be lunch time. What d'you say?'

'Fine. I could do with a bit of a loosener after all that tension. Have to give me a start, though. Bound to be bloody out of touch.'

Bowditch went out, then stuck his head round the door.

'Couple of things. Shouldn't go wandering round the grounds again. Might get mistaken for a Jerry spy and shot.'

Taking off his pyjama jacket, still sitting up in bed, Peters grinned. 'Sentry reported me, did he? Quite right too. Chap was dead on the alert. My compliments to the guard commander. Don't worry, Tristram. I'll be careful how and where I walk. Scout's honour.'

'The other thing is that I've invited John Standish to join us for lunch. Sorry you and he didn't quite hit it off. Shame. Anyway, see you outside in ten minutes.'

After he had gone, Peters dressed slowly, his face thoughtful. That small back room of doubt was still nagging away at him.

A quick shave, wincing as he nicked himself under the lip. Then, shrugging away his worries, he went out to join Bowditch in the fresh air.

The morning pursuits of John Standish were nothing like as healthy as those of Peters, but they were just as strenuous. Mrs. Protheroe had woken him up herself at nine, with a loaded breakfast tray.

Four fat pork sausages jostled half a dozen crisp rashers of back bacon. With the rinds cut off, as he always liked it. On a golden slice of fried bread, *three* sunny eggs lay companionably together. A couple of tomatoes completed the vision.

A silver rack of toast and china bowls of marmalade and strawberry preserve sat in the corner of the tray, with a dish of best butter. A steaming jug of coffee was already on the side of the table, with cream and sugar.

He sat up, rubbing sleep from the edges of his eyes. Mrs. Protheroe draped a cotton robe over his bare shoulders and plumped herself comfortably on the side of the bed.

Standish gave her a smacking kiss on the cheek. 'You're fantastic. Thanks. Christ knows how I'm going to plough my way through this lot. Incidentally, your little girl was a treat. Where's she gone?'

'She had an early morning appointment with a gentleman

who doesn't take kindly to being kept waiting.'

He paused with a forkful of sausage halfway to his mouth. "Not old ...?' and he gave a quick impression of a well-known politician. Mrs. Protheroe laughed and nodded. 'Well, I'm damned! Dirty old sod. She'll be wasted on him.'

While she chatted to him, he struggled on with the mountain of food. Most of it severely rationed.

A sudden thought occurred to him. 'Did you ring the Savoy Garage to make sure the Bentley was ready? Smashing. I've got bags of time. Lunch with Tristram isn't till two. Bloody uncivilized hour. Honestly, I just can't finish all this toast.'

'You ought to eat it all, John. I've never seen you looking so thin as you did last night. Oh!' Her hand went to her mouth as she realized what she'd said.

'Last night! You were at your bloody spy-hole again! Weren't you? You'll never get to heaven, Mrs. Protheroe.'

He wagged a finger at her. 'Naughty, naughty.'

When he heard feet coming nearer to his cell, Cybultna stopped his movement and lay still. The feet stopped outside his door, and the small observation slit grated open. An eye blocked off the light from the corridor.

A truncheon thudded on the door and a voice shouted at him. He opened his eyes and coughed. To show he was still alive. The eye went away and the slit closed. The feet marched slowly away, fading into the distance.

He waited until the silence had crept back again. Then, he began to work again. Steadily and perseveringly.

The wheel of the Bentley juddered as Standish swung her round on to the Great Cambridge Road, heading for his appointment with Bowditch. As it was the middle of the week, and near the middle of the day, there wasn't much traffic about. He opened her up and the speedometer touched eighty on the straight stretch between Cheshunt and Broxbourne.

He dived down into the dip and then up again towards Hoddesdon, the needle still quivering near seventy. Suddenly, without the least warning, a dog ran out of a side turning, about a hundred yards ahead. In such situations, his brain reacted for him and he had already made the decision not to risk a human life just to save a dog.

When another factor altered that decision. A little girl, barely four years old, darted after the dog. By now, the Bentley was much closer than one hundred yards, and the alternatives open were reduced to one. Biting his lip, he twisted the wheel sharply to the right, then back to the left. This had the effect of putting a kink in the car's movement forward, slewing it on to the wrong side of the road, missing the dog's head by inches and then back to miss the paralysed girl by the same distance.

He was just about to say a prayer to his own personal deity for keeping the road clear from oncoming traffic, when he felt the nearside wheel just clip the raised kerb. With a passing interest, Standish noted vaguely that he could still clearly hear the screaming of the mother of the little girl, who stood untouched in the centre of the main road.

'Silly bitch!' he thought. 'Should have kept her off the road in the first place.' The heavy car rocked as the tyre burst, and the rear end of the car dropped and bounced. 'And her fucking dog!' he thought, sitting helplessly as he felt the tail begin to spin round.

At that speed, there wasn't anything he could do that would make any material contribution to the final result. He made the gesture of steering into the spin, trying to brace himself at the same time for the inevitable.

The bang, when it did come, wasn't all that spectacular. Moving diagonally, the Bentley neatly removed a bicycle from the edge of the kerb. Mounted the pavement, brushed against a pillar-box, and entered smoothly through the front window of a haberdashery shop.

Standish ducked as he saw the impact coming, and most of

the splintered glass flew over his head, or showered over his tweed sports jacket. A cascade of ribbons splashed colourfully over the bonnet of the car, and a box of cotton reels landed neatly on the passenger seat.

Far back down the road, he could still hear the sound of the woman screaming. Apart from that, his spectacular entry into Hoddesdon seemed to have gone largely unnoticed. It was so quiet that he could even hear the drip of water from the burst radiator. He found that his nose was bleeding a little from a collision with the instrument panel. There was a rack of linen handkerchiefs right up against his elbow, so he took one and staunched the flow.

Somewhere above, he heard a door open, and steps moving along a landing. The barrel of a sporting shotgun suddenly appeared round the back stairs and a quavering voice said: 'Hande hoch, you Nazi bastard!'

The gun was followed by a small man, in his seventies, wearing an enormous pair of spectacles, held together by sticking plaster. When he saw Standish still sitting in the wrecked car, he nearly dropped the gun. 'Bloody hell! Couldn't you have parked on the highway, like other people?'

After a deal of explanations, both to the shop-owner and to the local police, Standish managed to get away. Arrangements were made with the local garage to remove the Bentley and do what had to be done. The policeman, when he heard Standish's destination, offered to lay on transport to get him there, but it would take a bit of time.

So, he rang through and left a message with one of Bowditch's assistants that he would be delayed and wouldn't be there for the noon broadcast, but would be there in ample time for lunch. He hoped. He was told that Bowditch was busy in a meeting, but would be told as soon as he was finished.

'Tell him I hope he wins – whatever he's playing.'

The aide was very cool. 'I'll give him your message, Mr. Standish, as soon as he's finished – his meeting.'

In Paris, Marreq was just waking up. His garotte cord had a thin wire core, and the pimp had an unusually fragile neck. Because he'd wanted to get back fast for his fix, Marreq hadn't bothered to wash. He was disgusted to find that his hair and face were dappled and sticky with blood.

At the S.O.E. house, Bowditch had been given the message from his assistant immediately he came off the squash court. To his considerable chagrin, Peters had beaten him in three out of the four games they'd played.

He was disappointed that Standish wouldn't be there for the report, but he knew – as did Standish – that there was no question at all of there being an alteration in the time of his man's broadcast. To set up the short-wave radio and send the coded message would take over a quarter of an hour, of which the greater part was devoted to the actual sending. The Germans had listening posts in all occupied cities, and they would immediately try and trace the source of the illicit communication. Noon it had been agreed, and noon it would be. Unless something had come to prevent him sending.

Peters had showered first, while Bowditch was talking to his aide. By the time Tristram got into the small, steamy changing-room, he was already half-dressed.

While he washed, Bowditch shouted him the news: 'Just heard Standish is going to be a bit late. Had a bit of a bang in his Bentley in Hoddesdon on the way here. Swerved to avoid a child apparently.'

'Good heavens! Not hurt I trust?'

'No. He should be here by about one.'

'Jolly good. Always was a bit of a lucky beggar.'

'Perhaps.' The steam grew thicker as Bowditch turned the temperature control as far round as it would go. 'By the way, Leslie, what time do you make it?'

'Ten minutes to twelve, old boy. Jolly nearly high noon. Time for you to be off for your meeting, what? I'll just potter about the place till it's time for the doc to check my ticker.

Then it'll be me for a big plate of that splendid roast beef. Keep my place warm, won't you, old boy, if I'm unavoidably detained? These medical chaps are never on time, you know.'

The police car was late, after chasing a suspected German paratrooper, who turned out to be a vicar from Norfolk doing some bird-watching. 'Better to be too careful, than not careful enough,' was Standish's only comment.

They took him along the quiet lanes, and over the railway line at Stanstead Abbotts. When they got to the end of the village high street, where the main road curves sharply between two old pubs, Standish asked them to drop off, so that he could stretch his legs by walking the rest of the way.

He climbed over a stile, and strode out across the fields. After the crash there had been a certain amount of tension in his body, and he knew from past experience that the best way to relax himself was a good long walk. He blanked out the memory of the accident, and concentrated on the country – the smells and the sounds. Tao Chu-wen had taught that peace could be found in the ways of men, but the greatest peace lay in the ways of Nature.

In about twenty minutes he came to the wire fence that marked the eastern perimeter of the establishment. He picked up a stick and banged it on the wire. Within a couple of minutes there was a patrol on the spot. He explained who he was and what his business was, and they directed him to a gate four hundred yards away.

Then, he was escorted to the main house by one of the armed guards, who was commendably careful to keep Standish a few paces in front of him. What he failed to do was search him. Fortunately, for, tucked in his belt, fully-loaded, was his stolen Luger.

And that might have been a little difficult to explain.

It was twelve twenty-five.

Before they reached the headquarters, Standish saw Bowditch come down the front steps and start to walk slowly over towards the medical hut, a hundred yards or so away on the other side, set among a small grove of pine trees. Hearing Standish shout, he turned round. For a moment, Standish thought he was going to ignore him, for he hesitated a long time before waving back.

'Hello, John, you made it all right then.'

'No, I was killed in the crash and this is merely an astral projection of me that's come to warn you about your wicked life.'

'Yes.' A pause. 'What the hell did you say?'

Standish looked at him closely. 'What's wrong, Tristram? You look as though you've had bad news. Didn't your man in Warsaw get through?'

'Oh, yes. Yes, he got through, all right. On the dot and clear as a bell.'

'Well?'

'Well, what?'

'For God's sake Tristram; either tell me what's up or don't. It's up to you. But don't stand there like a bloody fool. Come on.'

Bowditch still stood there, like a man involved in some abstruse mental arithmetic. As though he'd finally reached the solution, he faced Standish with his normal manner.

'Sorry. I think we should go for a walk, you and I. There're one or two things I've got to tell you.'

And he led the way off the gravel path, between the ornamental flower beds, towards the trees. On the way, they passed close to the green-painted hut with the sign 'Medical Officer' outside it. As they went past, there was a rapping on the window.

Standish turned and saw Peters waving and gesticulating to them. Bowditch took no notice, but called over a sergeant from by the hut. He took him a little distance away and Standish was unable to hear what was said. The sergeant saluted and marched smartly off. Bowditch gave a reassuring sort of wave to Peters and rejoined Standish.

Together they strolled among the trees. Neither broke the silence. They reached a small mound, looking down into a valley.

'Peaceful, isn't it? You'd hardly think there was a war on, would you? See that pine tree there, the dead one? Funny business that. My unarmed combat chap is red-hot on archaeology; always going to dig up remains and bits of old bone. He says there's a tumulus under that tree. Sort of a burial mound for some old Saxon king. Keeps asking permission to blow it open with a Mills bomb. Course, I won't let him. Know what he said? Reckons that the old king has drawn all the life out of the pine tree. Sucked it dry. Getting ready to rise again. Eh?'

Standish looked across the wood, watching the flight of a wood pigeon as it lurched out of the trees. Wanting to end it, he turned to Bowditch. 'Tell me, Tristram.'

'Our man in Warsaw. Totally reliable. Thorough. Came through right on time.'

'And?'

He looked him in the eyes, knowing how it would hit home. 'Peters has been a double agent. He betrayed most of his group to the Gestapo. The raid was a front. They picked him up to try and locate more Underground men in their prison. They never expected us to try and spring him like that.'

There was no reaction from Standish. His face was quite expressionless.

Bowditch went on. 'Funny business. He did it for money, yet it seems that it was the Gestapo who betrayed him in turn to the Poles. I suppose they thought they'd had their use from him.'

Standish's voice was bitter. 'Neumann! He'd betray his own mother if it suited him. One day ... So it was money. Fucking money? Not ideology. Not fear. Not pain. Just money. What's happened in Warsaw? What about Zbigniev and Anna?'

'They picked up the father, but there doesn't seem to be any news of the girl. Our man's got a contact who works actually inside Gestapo headquarters. Plucky kid by all accounts. Anyway, she said that there was an odd call to Neumann a few days ago. From Paris.'

Leaning his head against the cool bark of a birch tree, Standish sounded hopeless. 'Peters. When he got away from me. Tristram, what the hell happens to Warsaw now?'

'Well, that's about the only bright thing. The Poles have a fanatical hatred of the Hun, and our man is recruiting like mad. So, in that respect it wasn't that disastrous.'

His eyes flaming with a cold fire, he turned on Bowditch. 'Fuck you, Tristram! Look at the men and women who died in this operation. The dozens that rat betrayed. The lives that were risked. That lives that have been wrecked by that . . . And, Zbigniev. That's the worst. One of my own.'

'Yes, that's about the worst. Apparently, Cybultna knew more about the reformed Resistance than anyone else. Neumann will find some way to break him. Perhaps he has the girl. It's been a bloody mess. At least the Warsaw group is still functioning, unless Cybultna gives in. And you're safe. And we know Peters is a traitor.'

'Zbigniev won't give in. He'd rather die. What happens to Peters?'

It was some time before Bowditch answered. 'One other thing our man said, John.'

'Don't try and stall with me. What happens to Peters?'

'I'm not bloody stalling. Look, John, don't you think that this has hurt me as well? And, we've got to clean it all up. Let me tell you my bit of brighter news first. Our man said that the Germans are having a deal of trouble in Poland setting up their economy. Someone's flooded the country with some rather good forgeries of high value notes, overstamped with the German markings for use in Poland.'

'Good old, Jean. At least *he* did something without cocking it up.'

'As for Peters. There are several alternatives. He could be court-martialed. We could just arrange for him to be held somewhere and tried in secret. There might be an accident.'

'Bad for you if it all came out, wouldn't it, Tristram? What you mean is that you wouldn't mind that much if I did something about Peters for you. Wipe your arse clean. I bet you've arranged for me to have a fair run at him. Haven't you?'

Bowditch looked at him, and his voice was hard. 'John, he is my man and I would arrange it myself. But, it would help me if you were to erase him from our files. And, I think there must be a debt or two for you to pay off.'

It had been hard at first, digging the point of the pin through his own flesh. Gouging at the veins in the wrist, trying to keep them open and the blood flowing. The fingers on his left hand were too badly shattered for him to be able to operate effectively on his right wrist.

Also, it had to be done while lying still on his back under that sparse blanket. Forcing the body to keep still enough when the guard came round to peer through the Judas-window in the door. To be alive, so that he didn't come in and find the blood spreading through the clothes and soaking into the mattress.

His lips moved in a constant prayer as the point dug in and across. He knew that if he stopped too soon, or became unconscious too early, the blood might clot and congeal, and his body would do its best, despite his wishes, to keep him alive.

'Hail Mary, full of grace.' The point of the pin catching among the tendons and slipping from his hand. Fumbling to get it back.

'Blessed is the fruit of thy womb, Jesus.' Warm blood on his chest and stomach; rubbing at the upper arms, trying to chafe them and keep the circulation going. His life slowly draining away.

'Now and at the hour of our death.' Grinning at the thought that he was cheating Neumann. Going to join Maria. And Jerzy and Andrzej. Once he fell asleep and woke to find that the blood no longer flowed. The night passed slowly.

'If you don't mind, I think it might be easier if I strolled back first, round the back of the house, and engaged one or two people in chat. I'll stay close, so that I can get to you fast. Just say he attacked you.'

'Don't worry, Tristram. You get your hands washed.'

He turned and walked away. When he was at the edge of the covert, he looked back. 'Thank you John.'

Standish just waved a weary hand in acknowledgement. He didn't blame Bowditch. It was the best way, after all. He suddenly felt tired and grubby. After this was over, he'd go up north for a few days. Then, maybe, he'd try and get in touch with Jean again and maybe go back to ... No, that was looking to the past. All that was over.

Bloody Lobkowitz again. 'The living should bury the dead. But, the living should not then live all their time by the grave.'

He felt inside his jacket, and eased off the safety catch on his pistol. To be on the safe side, he allowed Bowditch three minutes to get on his way, then began his own, slow return.

Among the trees it was cool, and the heat of the sun, when he came out on to the top field, struck at him like a physical blow. He approached the medical hut from the opposite side, where there were no windows.

Just as he got to the doorway, the heat became so much that he stopped and pulled out a handkerchief. While he was wiping the sweat from his face and neck, he heard a voice close behind.

'Bloody hot, innit sir?'

It was the corporal who'd escorted him from the perimeter gate. He gave him a friendly grin, hoping he'd go away. But, the soldier was encouraged and came over.

'Feeling a bit Tom and Dick?'

For a moment, his mind on a death, Standish didn't realize what on earth the man meant. Then, the penny dropped.

'Oh, sick! No. Just slipping in to see if the M.O. has anything for a bit of a headache.'

'It's this heat, sir. Shirtsleeve order for weeks now it's been.

They say it's nearly ninety in the shade, today. Still, mustn't grumble, eh?'

'No, I suppose not.' He heard the clock in the village strike one. Peters would be getting suspicious if nobody showed up.

'Last Whit Monday, I took the wife and the nippers down to Clacton for a day. Had a spot of leave. Well, you see I missed out on my leave that I normally take at the end of September. Bloody 'itler. The kids were choked off as well. Instead of a good time at the seaside, they were evacuated to some dead-end dump in the country, miles from anywhere.'

'Corporal, I'm sorry, but I'm a bit pushed for time.'

'Nearly done, sir. Where was I?'

'On your way to Clacton on Whit Monday.'

'Right. Well, it was a bloody scorcher. The chara was packed out. Cyril – he's the youngest – was sick on the missus's new coat. She lost her purse and started crying. I cut me foot on a broken bottle. Then, when we got home, we listened to Churchill on the wireless. And, what did he say?'

Standish clenched his fists in anger. Then, he realized that the soldier was nearly at the end of his narrative. So, he forced a smile. 'I wasn't in the country then. What did he say?'

'He said: "I have nothing to offer you but blood, toil, tears and sweat." And I said to the wife. "Blimey, he must have been on our chara to Clacton today." Because he seemed to know what it'd been...'

'I get it, corporal.' And he laughed, genuinely amused.

The soldier grinned at him. 'Right, sir. Won't keep you. Hope the M.O. has something for your head.'

Standish acknowledged his salute with a 'Cheerio', then walked into the medical hut.

He found himself in a small ante-room, with a door in the far corner. Behind it, he heard steps and a voice. 'Is that the doc? I say, old boy, I thought you weren't coming. I'd begun to give you...'

His words drifted into quiet as he saw Standish come in and close the door behind him. He moistened his lips, and rubbed his finger across his mouth in a nervous gesture.

Standish pulled out the gun.

Peters looked at it, and all the life seemed to leave him. Like a puppet with faulty strings, he sat down heavily on a cane chair.

'How do you know?'

'Bowditch has a new man in Warsaw. Done a good job. He found out and radioed it through today. Everything.'

'Do you know why? Blair was right. Everybody has some weakness. Mine is just weaker than most. I like money. I contacted that sinister Neumann fellow. He paid me well. But, he promised that the names I gave him wouldn't be really hurt. If they were spies, they'd be shot. I mean, old boy, that's fair enough. He promised me there'd be a fair trial. Anyone innocent would go free.'

The mattress was sodden with blood. The body holds between nine and ten pints, and man can live with surprisingly little of that. Cybultna's breathing had become very shallow and his pulse was faint and irregular. But, his broken fingers still held the bent safety-pin. Still drew it steadily through the shambles of his left wrist. Kept the blood trickling.

Slower and shower.

Because Herr Stürmbannführer Neumann believed in giving people time to think things over, Cybultna was left in his cell until lunch-time. Then a young S.S. trooper came in and found him asleep. Kicked him. Again, harder. Then pulled off the thin blanket.

And vomited at the bloody carnage of the old man's body.

'Be with us now, and at the hour of our death.'

Standish squeezed the trigger of the Luger slowly, and almost regretfully. The heavy bullet hit Peters plumb in the centre of his right knee. It shattered the delicate joint, breaking the bottom of the femur, and the patella, tearing the ligaments into shreds.

Peters cried out in shock, the force of the blow sending him spinning from the chair onto the floor. He tried to sit up, to hold the ruined leg together with his hands. Somehow smooth the pain away.

The second bullet tore apart the right elbow, again throwing him on his back. Blood and bone sprayed across the polished wood. Standish stepped nearer, moving the gun, trying to hold his aim as Peters threshed and screamed.

The third and fourth shots were aimed at the left knee and the left elbow. The one hit, the other missed by a fraction, breaking the fore-arm instead.

Like a mortally-wounded spider, Peters flopped helplessly at his feet, finger-nails breaking as he tried to scratch his way along. The whole time, he kept up a thin, barely audible scream.

Four bullets gone and four remaining. Two went into the traitor's stomach and groin. As he rolled, the floor about him grew beslobbered with his blood. Where bullets had gone clean through him, the smooth wood was chipped and scarred, with red-soaked splinters standing up at ugly angles.

By now Standish could hear voices outside. Men running. Tristram's voice above the rest. 'Let me through. The rest of you stay outside.'

The crash of the outer door, then the awareness that Bowditch was standing watching. Peters, still moving, moaning more quietly, twitching.

Standish stood still and watched the life slipping out of the man at his feet. And he remembered an old man in Warsaw and his daughter. One of Peter's hands, bloody, brushed his foot, held it desperately. He fired the seventh bullet and watched dispassionately as the hand exploded into a blot of pulped flesh and white bone.

'My God! Standish! My God! My God! John! No!'

The gun still in his hand, he turned round and faced Bowditch. 'That's what it's all about, Tristram. Thought you'd like a chance to see for yourself.'

Then, scarcely looking, he fired the last shot through the forehead of the mewing creature that had been Leslie Peters, and made it still.

His eyes locked with Bowditch, he walked wearily to him. As he passed, he put the warm Luger into his hand. Saying nothing, for there really was nothing left to say.

And walked out into the hot, sunny afternoon.

Five days later, Standish sat by the wireless in his country house and listened to the words of Winston Churchill.

Alone.

It had been a speech about defeat. Yet it ended:

'We shall not flag or fail. We shall go on to the end, we shall fight in France, we shall fight on the seas and oceans, we shall fight with growing confidence and growing strength in the air, we shall defend our island, whatever the cost may be, we shall fight on the beaches, we shall fight on the landing grounds, we shall fight in the fields and in the streets, we shall fight in the hills; we shall never surrender.'

KING OIL 30p

Max Catto

The voice of my beloved! he cometh,
Leaping upon the mountains, skipping upon
the hills. SONG OF SOLOMON

Frank Dibbler, already a millionaire who wants to be an oil king and become founder of a dynasty that will perpetuate his name in the future industrial America that he foresees, chooses as his wife the daughter of a Spanish grandee, taking her on the long hazardous journey from the genteel pomp of Seville to the vast, untamed ranch-land of Texas.

This epic yarn is Max Catto's finest and most gripping novel.

THE FAMILY 40p

Leslie Waller

Truly great novels about the Mafia are few and far between. *The Family* is not only the most recent but one of the very, very best. The *New York Times* called it "a jumbo entertainment, full of everything" and drew attention to the book's shattering combination of big business, violence, raw sex, protest and comment on the richest society in the history of the world. It is a dramatic and engrossing story that exposes a new breed of gangster less concerned with strong-arm tactics than with financial manipulation. Woods Palmer, chief executive of America's biggest banking empire, becomes the pawn in an operation of a naked ruthless power that only the Mafia's mighty, complex machine can wield with such effectiveness and shameless brutality.